TORN

The third book in the best selling
Demon Kissed Series

www.DemonKissed.com

Join over 40,000 fans on facebook!
www.facebook.com/DemonKissed

TORN

H.M. WARD

Laree Bailey Press

Laree Bailey Press, 4431 Loop 322, Abilene, TX 79602

Printed in the United States of America
First Printing: August 2011
10 9 8 7 6 5 4 3 2 1

Library of Congress Cataloging-in-Publication Data

Ward, H.M.
Torn / H.M. Ward – 1st ed.
 p. cm.
ISBN 978-0615559360

Other Books By H.M. Ward

DEMON KISSED

Cursed

Satan's Stone

*Thank you to my
Super awesome husband!
I love you like crazy!*

*Thank you to the
Awesome fans who loved
Demon Kissed
From the very beginning.*

Demon Kissed
I. WAR.

PAINTING OF IVY TAYLOR

TORN

CHAPTER ONE

Sometimes a single decision can result in a cascade of actions that you never intended. This was one of those times. I'd never once thought about ending my life, not even when I felt like there was no way to survive the pain of losing my sister. I was a robot back then, awaking every morning, reminding myself to breathe, and that tomorrow would come. Somehow I expected everything to resolve itself if I could just survive the motions of getting through the day. But, somehow my life had deteriorated into this one horrifying moment, where everything hinged on me and my love for this boy.

It wasn't only my fate that depended on this one decision—it was the fate of mankind. Until then, I didn't see how my affection for Collin could possibly condemn the world and unleash the apocalypse, but now I did. Collin's prone form breathed silently next to me after Kreturus took possession of his body. The ancient demon's dark shapeless form entered Collin's limp body through lesions that were inflicted by the lesser demons. In one horrifying moment, my world had changed. There was nothing that could have prepared me for this moment, because there was no preparation for a decision like this.

My life or his.

And whose life was it? Whose life was I taking? Was he Kreturus or Collin? Had the demon invaded his body and taken over his mind? Or was this Collin laying there helpless. There was no way for me to know. Not without waiting for Collin to wake up. And no matter what, that was a terrible idea. If Collin were awake, he could talk to me. His sweet voice would assure me that everything was all right and that we could be together now.

There is no way I'd ever forget what I'd seen, that Kreturus was actually inside of him. But, how could I kill the one I loved? He was part of me. I'd die if I plunged the fang into his chest. No, this was the only way. And I knew this was my one and only chance to end this horrifying confrontation between me and Kreturus, and that I needed to do it before Collin awoke.

An internal signal erupted in my mind telling me what to do—what I had to do. If I removed the pivotal player from the game, then the game would be over. There would be no one left to carry on my role as the Prophecy One and cause the end of the world. There would be no more anything. I'd be removed from scenario, crippling Kreturus' plans. This was like a game of chess—kill the queen and the king would be vulnerable.

Swallowing hard, I pushed back the fear that was choking me. The only object that could destroy me was gripped tightly in my fist. The sapphire serum within the silver fang could destroy both angels and demons. Its poison did not discriminate. It was lethal no matter who touched it.

The fang was poised over my heart, and ready to strike.

There was no hesitation in my swing. I would not be the girl in the prophecy, and this was the only way to ensure it would never come to pass. Without my tainted blood there would be no one to free Kreturus. Without me, the prophecy would dissolve and cease to exist. I glanced at Collin as my fingers curled tighter around the silver tooth. Every muscle in my body flexed in anticipation. The point of the fang needed to pierce my heart. It was the only way for the poison within it to kill me instantly. The moment it struck my heart, the venom would be pumped throughout my body. In one heart beat I would die. In one heart beat the prophecy would end. I breathed deeply, one last breath, as every ounce of rage, every broken hope and shattered dream came to the front of my mind.

And I swung.

It was an action that I would undo, if I could. It was this act of martyrdom that created a ripple effect in the pond of my eternally screwed-up life. This one selfless act is what ultimately led to the corruption and demise of mankind. You see, the fang didn't pierce my heart as I'd intended. Everything happened so quickly that it's difficult to say exactly what happened. But, as the fang swung toward me an ear piercing scream erupted and I was knocked to the floor. The tooth collided with something mid-swing and missed its original target. Instead, the fang caught the skin between my breasts, as a hand tried to stop me. But, the force and speed of my strike was too powerful to stop, so the silver fang sliced a U across my chest and up into my shoulder. Crimson flowed from the wound in the wake of the silver fang. It cut through me like I was made of butter. My flesh hissed as if it were burned. The blue sapphire serum leaked from the fang and mingled together with my blood, as I screamed in utter agony clutching my chest.

My words were incoherent screams at first, as I doubled over. I didn't know what happened. How did I miss? But as my senses fought for control through the searing pain of the poisoned fang, I saw what caused my aim to falter.

Collin.

His blue eyes were wide and panic stricken. He was speaking, but I couldn't understand what he was saying. The pain was too intense to focus on anything else. His words sounded like babble, and made no sense to me. As I writhed on my side he reached for me. Fear clutched my stomach in unrelenting waves as his hands extended toward my wound with an expression of terror on his face. He kneeled over me with tears streaming down his face. I finally understood what he was saying. His unfathomable words suddenly had meaning.

He was screaming, "Ivy! What did you do?"

I recoiled, afraid of his touch—afraid of his words. My heart raced as terror shot through me. It was him. That demonic version of the boy I loved. He made me miss. His fist had collided with my hand and sent the fang on a shallow, but deadly path across my chest. My lungs sucked in air with quick pants as I tried to endure the pain. It didn't matter that the fang didn't pierce my heart. The end result would be the same, but this was a much more painful way to die. Instead of instant death, this would be a slow painful demise.

Pulling my bloodied hands away from my chest, I clawed at the ground, backing away from him. "Don't touch me!" The voice that rang in my ears sounded foreign even though I felt it rip from my throat in a panicked cry.

"Ivy," he pleaded, "Ivy, let me help you. Please." The urgency in voice said he knew my wound was fatal. He knew what I'd done, but the expression in his eyes said he didn't know why. His blue eyes were wide with fear as he tried to help me. The same touch I once longed for was now terrifying.

I felt like I couldn't breathe. Beads of sweat formed on my brow and trickled down my temples. The poison was no longer isolated in my chest, and I could feel it working its way slowly down my arms. As Collin reached for me again, I shrank back from his touch. He wasn't Collin anymore—he was Kreturus. I didn't want the demon near me. I couldn't stand the thought of him touching me with Collin's hands.

Sweat was pouring off of me as I became increasingly lightheaded. "I don't need your help! I know what you wanted me for and you can't have me.

There's no point in trying to take Collin from me, you demonic bastard! You lose! My powers die with me!"

He didn't back away from me while I screamed at him. Instead he glanced around like he thought I was talking to someone else. Someone he couldn't see. Confusion, mingled with desperation, spread across his face, "Who are you talking to? Who do you think you see? Ivy, talk to me!" He tried to reach for me again, but he stopped when he saw the pain on my face, as I tried to move away from him. He sat on his knees, not knowing what to do with his hands, looking utterly helpless. His voice was weak, "What happened? Why would you do this?"

Every muscle in my body was flexed as I tried to manage the pain and failed. My eyes shut tight as I clenched my teeth. I felt like my flesh was burning where the fang had torn open my skin. The sapphire serum burned like other forms of evil magic, but differently than effonation. It felt like acid leaking into my body in a steady slow stream. Through gritted teeth I uttered, "Don't act like you're not you. I saw you possess him. You're trying to use him against me." I glanced up into his eyes and swallowed hard. The expression on Collin's face almost made me believe that he wasn't Kreturus, and that he sincerely had no idea what happened. But the poison slowly spreading through my body wouldn't let me forget who he really was. There was no way that demon wasn't in him. I knew what I saw.

"I swear to God, Ivy—this isn't what you think," his voice was faint. A shallow breath left his body as he rammed his fingers through his hair. "It's not what you think." His voice trembled. Tears streaked his face as he looked down at the ground. Hopelessness engulfed him.

My head was spinning with feverish pain. Was it possible that I was wrong? Was it possible that this was really Collin? The pain on his face—the look of terror in his eyes was real. Maybe it was Collin. I blinked hard trying to focus. Wooziness made it difficult to think, but I had to know.

"Prove it," I whispered. My eye lids were growing heavy. The sapphire serum burned its way through most of my body. There wasn't an inch of me that wasn't scorched from within. Some areas of my skin started smoking in thin blue wafts. I didn't have much time left. "Prove you're Collin and only Collin."

He glanced up at me. "There are no words that will convince you of that. You saw something…I don't know what, but it terrified you into thinking this was the only way to prevent the prophecy." Pain that I couldn't imagine had devoured my body in a matter of minutes, and I saw every speck of that pain reflected in Collin's eyes.

Clearing my throat, I said, "Kreturus is inside of you. Or he is you. I don't know which." The room was spinning. Kreturus did go into Collin, but I expected him to be different somehow and he wasn't. It bothered me, but I couldn't understand why. Perhaps it was the venom rotting my brain. A weak sliver of a voice slid from my lips, "It doesn't matter now."

Tears were streaming down his face, and his blue eyes were burning bright. He bit his lips as if he didn't know what to say. My eyelids drooped, but I couldn't take my eyes from his. Finally, he said, "I know you don't want me to touch you. I know you're afraid. But I can help you. I can slow the poison. Ivy, I have to…" with that he reached for me. His fingers pressed against my chest and I screamed.

His hands felt like lead, increasing the agony I already felt. I don't know if it was a physical reaction to Kreturus or if the additional pain was from the wound, but his touch intensified the agony. His hands pressed on my bloodied chest, as he uttered words that I couldn't understand. Whatever he was saying, it wasn't English. I didn't recognize it at all. More foreign words fell from him lips, as his fingers traced the wound across my chest.

What did he say? Was he really trying to heal me? Could he do that? I didn't know, but I did know that I had to get away. I'd made my decision—this wasn't

Collin. It was Kreturus. And I couldn't risk whatever the demon was planning to do. It was unbearable watching him looking at me the way Collin used to. It was the same expression he wore so many times, but intensified—the sorrow behind his eyes, the determination of his shoulders, and the confidence on his lips. He seemed so lost and frightened. It made me feel like I was the air that he needed to breathe and I had to be close to sooth him. But, there was no soothing him now. There was no nice way to end this.

My body was too weak to fight my way out of his grasp. He was determined to heal me and I was determined to stop him. There was only one way to do it. If I acted quickly, I could effonate to the one place where no one would follow me. It was the one place I knew for certain that I could die alone.

I fixated on the place in my mind, fighting back the fatigue that was pawing at me. As heat seared through me, I glanced up into his eyes one more time. They held more words than he could have ever said. Kreturus chose well. Collin was the only one who could have tempted me. He was the only one I wanted, and now I'd never have him. His thoughts pushed at my mind trying to convince me to rest and let him slow the poison. I felt his desperation, but couldn't give in. I'd done the only thing I knew that would stop the prophecy.

Collin didn't realize what I was doing until I whispered, "You meant everything to me. I love you. Good-bye, Collin." As I focused on the ruby ring and effonated away, I heard Collin screaming my name.

CHAPTER TWO

I appeared in the place I'd wanted, the place where no one would find me—the Lorren. Ironically, I'd be safe in the ancient tomb. No one could follow me here because they'd never seen the inside of this horrible place. The only three people to have ever survived the Lorren's snare were Shannon, Eric, and me. And I blasted Shannon back to New York, and Eric...well, Eric was hunting Shannon. Collin might try to use the bond to find me. That thought occurred to me, but he'd never locate me before the Lorren tempted him to death. No, he wouldn't come.

I'd die alone.

Staggering, I reached out for the golden wall. My legs couldn't support my weight and I collapsed on the rust colored stain near the exit, with my face pressed to the cold, golden floor. With drugged eyes too heavy to remain open much longer, I stared at the stain. It was the place Eric had died. It was the place I'd made an unforgiveable error and given my first demon kiss. I traced my finger over the bloodstain as silent sobs bubbled up from deep within me. That smear of blood was the embodiment of my worst failure. It was the foretelling of the evil that was growing inside of me.

I didn't retreat to a place that would allow me to die in peace. It was a place that reminded me that my decision was right. The Lorren reminded me that I was what I was—the Prophecy One—and that I was dangerous. This place marked the death of the Ivy I was, the loss of my innocence as I drank my first soul. It didn't matter to me that Eric was dying. It didn't matter that I tried to save him and screwed up. That's exactly why I was so dangerous—I didn't give up. I kept trying and it was those attempts that seemed to push things over the edge. The look on Collin's face made me question my actions, but being in this place confirmed my original thoughts - I'd made the right choice.

As tears streaked my face, and puddled under my cheek, I closed my eyes. My entire body had grown numb as the poison spread throughout. My hands clutched my chest beneath me and were coated in warm blood from the laceration. I'd never given much thought to dying and wondered if the sleepiness that was tugging at me was death summoning me. It didn't matter what it was, because there was no more time to think about anything. There was no more time for regrets or worries. A wave of weariness that was too heavy to endure closed my eyes for me, and everything went black.

I fell into the nothingness, suspended in an inky, cold darkness. Pain didn't exist. For a brief moment, nothing happened. It felt more like I was trapped in a dream that was stuck on pause. I'm not certain how long I remained in that state. It was like I was aware of my soul, but had no control over my form. My body was gone—dissolved into the pitch-black nothingness.

After a while, the dreams started. Strange dreams. There was a dark-haired boy talking to me, but I didn't know what he was saying. He spoke and gestured that I should follow. His orange shorts had big white flowers printed on them. I wondered if he was going to go swimming. I liked swimming, but I didn't follow him, which seemed to piss him off.

Then, the dream shifted and the boy was older now. His hair darkened to black and words spilled out of his mouth like water. I swear I could see the words dangle through the air as he spoke to me. He said my name over and over again, and the letters I V Y poured over his lips and pooled at my feet. Before long, the dream shifted again.

I sat alone in the darkness, cross-legged on the floor. Slowly, I glanced around seeing nothing but a single flame flickering in the darkness. Rising to my feet I moved towards the light, but it moved farther and farther away. Panic flooded the dream and suddenly I was running—running towards the candle as it was being carried away. I had to find it. I had to stop it from leaving. But, it was already gone. I pressed my eyes closed, and blinking slowly, reopened them.

The dream changed and as my eyes focused in the dimly lit room I could see golden walls covered in flickering candlelight. My senses went into overdrive as the lightness I'd felt vanished. Confused, I blinked again and continued to look around. Where was I? I thought I was dead, but this looked like the Lorren. Fear pooled in the pit of my stomach. Spending eternity damned in the confines of the Lorren made me stomach twist. But, that's where I was. Golden jewel encrusted poppies lined the walls. This was definitely the Lorren, but it wasn't the place I'd fallen. There was a cold hard surface pressing against my back. My fingers pressed into the golden slab I was laying on. Someone must have moved me from the place I'd fallen. My mind was still foggy. Whether it was the after effects of the poison or death, I wasn't sure. I just knew that I should have been dead, and instead, I felt quite alive. Blood rushed through my heart, which was racing in my chest. The surreal feelings that had overcome me after I fell were gone. My body and my soul were glued together again, and my pain was nearly gone. My eyes flicked through the large room looking for answers. It became very clear that I was somewhere else within the evil maze of temptation. And someone was here with me.

The boy leaned over a work table with tiny tools, at the center of which was a single jeweled rose. Its stem and petals were deep blue, with the exception of a few petals, which gleamed bright silver. The boy crafting the rose was tall and slender. His black hair hung in his face as he worked, meticulously grasping the slender stem between callused fingers. A dingy black tee shirt hung two sizes too big to his body.

He spoke without turning towards me, "So, you're awake." It wasn't a question. He turned around to look at me. A shiver ran down my spine. There was something about him, something intimidating beyond anything I'd ever felt. His pale skin and dark hair seemed otherworldly and his brilliant green eyes shone like emeralds.

I tried to sit up, but my head felt like my skull was cracked open. Weakness limited my movements. Instead of responding, I moaned and closed my eyes.

The boy spoke again, "I wouldn't move around too much. You had a nasty wound there." He pointed at my chest. My hand rose to my breastbone and I slid my fingers across my chest. There was a long, thin welt on my skin. Before I could speak, he answered my question. "Yeah, there's a scar. But you're lucky. Very lucky. That crap almost killed you. But I knew how to save you." He twirled the blue rose between his fingers. It was an odd movement. He'd just been so careful with it that it seemed wrong for him to twirl it so carelessly. Maybe he didn't care if it shattered if it slipped between his fingers.

So this guy saved me. I stared at him wondering how that was possible. He was a scrawny nobody twirling flowers in the Lorren. My throat tightened as I wondered if that flower was someone. The Lorren's lined with flowers that were people who'd not made it out alive. The whole situation seemed too weird to be true, but here I was. So what happened? Who was this guy and why was he in the Lorren? And more importantly, why did he save me. He just stopped me from preventing the apocalypse. Irritation shot through me. Arrogance flowed off of him in waves, as he smirked smugly at me.

My voice rasped as I slowly sat up, holding my throbbing head, "You have no idea what you did." My voice was level and unfeeling. I didn't know how he healed me, who he was, or what to do next. Shit! This wasn't supposed to happen. I effonated to the Lorren because I was the only one who survived it. No one else could enter without the magic of the Lorren screwing with them and eventually killing them. And yet—here was black-haired boy looking at me in all his Goth glory.

"Yes, I think I do." He answered. He smiled that smug smile again, "You just made the biggest mistake of your life. And I fixed it." Walking towards me, he carelessly twirled the blue rose between his fingers.

I glared at him from my place on the golden slab. "Who are you? What'd you do to me?" I wished I was able to stand, but I couldn't move. My head felt large and too heavy to remain upright on top of my shoulders. It felt like a lead balloon and I was having issues holding it up. I blinked hard and felt the room sway. Apparently I swayed, because the boy caught me in his arms and laid me back down.

"Easy there. Quit trying to get up. You're too weak. And I'm not quite done yet." He reached for my neckline and I swatted at him, slapping his hands away.

"What are you doing? You can't grope me, you perv." I couldn't believe this was happening. This insane boy had revived me and was trying to grab a feel. My head throbbed so badly that I wanted to close my eyes and stop thinking. As it was, it felt like rusty gears scraping against each other in my brain just to form a sentence.

He laughed, shocked, and shook his head. "Don't flatter yourself. I'm using this to make a sieve and draw the poison out of you. Where'd you get this wound, anyway? It was pretty nasty." Feeling confused, I swatted him away again as he reached for my neckline. "I liked you better asleep." He frowned at me and folded his arms.

My jaw was hanging open. "I was dying. I wasn't asleep. And you screwed me over."

He laughed, "You mean you wanted to die? There's no way you're that stupid. I mean, I've heard things about the awesome Ivy Taylor, but that would be truly idiotic. There's no way you would have tried to kill yourself. " He slid up onto a golden ledge similar to the one I was laying on and looked at me.

I have no idea what expression was on my face, but his words made me pause. He knew who I was. And he seemed to think my death would be a bad thing. My eyes became narrow slits as I growled, "Don't pretend you know what you're talking about or what just happened to me. You don't know! You just came along and screwed it all up."

Slouching, he gestured toward my chest—ignoring my comments—and tilted the flower toward me. "Can I finish this or not?"

Glancing at him out of the corner of my eye, I pressed my lips tightly and didn't respond. The boy was leaning forward, dangling his legs over the edge of the golden slab he sat on. Suspicion raked me. Maybe I was horrible, but there is no way anybody who chose to be in the Lorren was up to anything good.

His words bounced around in my brain until I was asking myself questions; what did he do to draw out the poison? How did he do it? I didn't think it was possible. Everything I heard about sapphire serum said it was lethal. I never heard of someone removing the poison from infected blood, but I was new to all this. So maybe he could. But the thought that clattered the loudest as it bounced through my head was this one: why did he think that sacrificing myself was a mistake?

From his comments, he seemed to think it would be utterly stupid. And that I should have known better. But I didn't. There was no mistake in my mind – removing me from the equation was the only option. No more Ivy, meant no more prophecy. At least I thought it did, but now I wasn't so sure. Not with this arrogant boy sitting here inferring otherwise.

He stared at me until I finally nodded. Part of me was curious to see what he was going to do. The other part was tired of feeling the pain. And if I was going to finish what I started and impale myself with a Guardian fang again, I needed to know what he knew about the prophecy.

And me.

He slid off his perch and took long strides toward me. His green eyes locked with mine for a moment as he stood above me. It was intimidating.

He was intimidating. I just couldn't understand why. He was tall, but he was lanky. It wasn't his size or his appearance that put the fear of God into me. It was something else, but I had no idea what.

His emerald eyes finally broke away from mine before gazing down towards my chest. Flinching at his touch, he slid his fingers under my neckline slightly as he pulled it down and revealed a long scar. The scar formed a gash that marred my skin from the center of my breastbone up to my shoulder. The gentle scoop of the tank top I was wearing covered the entire scar.

His hand drifted to the beginning of the scar just below my neckline—to the place where the fang first pierced my skin at the top of my breast. That was the only part of the wound that still contained sapphire serum. I could see it. A faint blue line was buried deep inside of my skin.

The black-haired boy didn't glance up at me as he carefully placed a silver petal against my skin. His rough hands handled the flower delicately. His attention was solely fixated on the rose and the wound. As he touched the flower's stem to the only part of my wound that still contained sapphire serum, I could see the silver petals slowly soak up the blue. Streaks appeared in the silver, veining it in tiny intricate spider-webs through the metal petals. His fingers worked deftly, twirling the rose while touching it to my chest lightly.

Petal after petal veined and then turned blue. As the poison was drawn out of my body and into the rose, the pain that ravaged me subsided. My nails had bitten into my palms because I had my fists balled so hard. As the pain eased, I noticed the ache in my cramped fingers and the nail marks in my flesh.

It was uncomfortable to have this guy hovering over my exposed chest drawing out poison like that, but it seemed to be working. And he didn't try to feel me up. He didn't ask me about my missing bra, tattered clothing, or the blood stains that covered my outfit. Instead, he focused on his fingers and the flower, saying nothing while he worked. The flower twirled and slowly I felt better.

But, before the serum was completely gone, the process stopped. The blue veins drawing the poison out dried up before the rose was filled, leaving it with a single silver petal. The boy stopped twirling the rose. He lifted it from me and maneuvered it to try again.

I waited to see what would happen. But as I watched, nothing changed. It was like the stem broke and the silver rose had reached its poison threshold. He shook his head and lifted the flower away from my skin, flipping over the rose to look at the tip of the stem. He bit the side of his mouth, pulling his lips into an odd expression. Flipping the flower over again, he glared at me with those haunting eyes.

He blurted out what he was thinking without sugar-coating it, "What's wrong with you? What's wrong with your soul?"

CHAPTER THREE

Out of all the questions that I expected him to ask, that wasn't one of them. I visibly flinched. "What? Nothing." He was looking at me oddly. Not quite judgmental like the Martis, but still not a good look.

His brow creased, as he examined the rose between his fingers. "No, there is something definitely wrong with your soul." His gaze shifted from the rose to my horrified face. His voice was stern and certain. "This rose is made from Celestial Silver. I used it to draw out the sapphire serum. The rose holds the venom in its petals. The silver rose is the only thing that can hold the serum. Sapphire serum is poison and destroys everything it touches, except this." He spun the rose in his fingers. "It would have killed you. Once that stuff gets into your blood, the poison multiples and gets very difficult to draw out.

"When I found you, you were a lost cause. The venom had spread throughout your entire body and was messing with your brain. You were barely breathing. So I grabbed you and brought you back here. I knew that the poison likes silver—it's drawn to it the way an iron filing is drawn to a magnet. So when I touched the silver to your wound, it pulled out the sapphire serum, little by little, until there was only this small amount left. But, it's like I can't draw out this last bit of poison. It's as if your soul has been taken—like part of it is missing." He shook his head as if he didn't believe his own words.

I looked away embarrassed and asked, "Why would that matter?"

His eyebrow shot up into his hair line as he regarded me for a moment. "Because. It's not natural for a being to have part of her soul missing. Sure, souls can be ripped from the body, but when that happens, the part of the soul that was taken dies. It's just gone."

I stiffened, "A Valefar took most of my soul." That was true. Jake took almost all of it, but I had a feeling that wasn't what he was talking about. The entire conversation, and the look on his face, made me squirm.

Shaking his head he said, "No, that's different. A soul devoured by a Valefar dies. It goes to the Pool of Lost Souls for a reason—it's lost. A dead soul cannot be revived. It's dead. But that's not the case with you. The rose just can't do it. It's like part of your living soul is somewhere else, but that's impossible…" he arched an eyebrow staring at me, waiting for an explanation.

I squirmed under his gaze, and tried to sit up again. I managed to pull myself up slowly without falling over. The boy didn't help me. He just stared with a hard look on his face. I didn't like this guy interrogating me. Who was he anyway? He totally screwed up my plan and I sure as hell didn't want to stab myself again. It took more courage than I had the first time.

"Why isn't that possible?" I asked. "And who are you anyway? And stop looking at me like that!" His jaw was slack, and his mouth was hanging open slightly. He was shocked.

By me.

He pushed his hair behind his ear and shut his mouth. "It's not possible, because a soul can't be torn in pieces and remain alive. That's just it. Damage like that is deadly. There is no natural separation of part of the soul from the body. It's not like we can just tear it in two and put part of it somewhere else!"

Um, that was news to me, because that was exactly what I did. I had given a piece of my soul to Collin.

This kid was going to flip out if I told him. Instead I demanded, "Answer me. Who are you? Why'd you save me?"

The boy folded his arms and stared at me, equally stubborn. He didn't like my tone, but I really didn't care. I wasn't apologizing for it.

His expression hardened. "I saved you because I could. I assumed you wanted to avoid propelling the prophecy into motion, so I saved you. You can't die, not like this. Don't you see? Can't you tell what would have happened?" His voice became louder and louder as he spoke, yelling at me like I was an idiot. "Part of your soul is somewhere else. If you had died, your body would have died, and the remnant of your soul— wherever it is—would receive your powers. You have powers, right? The prophecy one is supposed to have great powers, and that's you. Killing yourself would have shifted all of your bad-ass power straight into that piece of soul that isn't inside of you anymore." He was quite for a moment. Thoughts were flying through his mind, and he began to speak them, putting the pieces together in front of me. "But, that piece of your soul is still alive... And for it to be alive, it has to be inside a living being—someone else. Ivy, did you give a piece of your soul away?" He looked horrified, as if there was no way I would ever do such a thing. His hard gaze and shocked expression didn't make me question my decision to give a piece of my soul to Collin, but it did make me feel ashamed.

I looked away sharply. "I had to." My voice was faint. "I did it to save someone. He would have died without it."

The black-haired boy studied me. "Who? Who has your soul inside of them? Who will inherit your powers when the poison spreads through your body?"

Coldness filled the pit of my stomach, as I realized the magnitude of what he was saying. If my body died and my soul ceased to exist in this body, a piece of me was left elsewhere. That person would absorb all my powers. They would naturally flow into the only remaining piece of soul. And the person who had it was possessed by a demon.

"Collin."

The boy arched his eyebrow at me and shook his head. "You're a hot mess, aren't you? Good God! No wonder why you're the one who causes this whole disaster. You have no idea what the hell you're doing!"

"Like you do?" I wanted to leave the Lorren, but I wasn't sure if I could stand, never mind find my way out again. Shit. I had to undo this. I had to get the sapphire serum out of my chest.

He looked incredulous; like I shouldn't dare challenge him. He was obviously a Valefar who'd made a hideout inside the Lorren. At first I thought he was an idiot, and then I realized that was something I would do and lost all of the bluster that I was ready to spew at him. Instead I asked again, "Who are you?"

He stared at me, with his emerald eyes locked on my face. He bit his bottom lip for a moment before answering. It seemed to be a nervous tic, a gesture that he didn't realize he had that surfaced when he was tense...or afraid.

Silence surrounded us until he finally told me. "I'm Lorren."

Annoyed, I felt my eyebrow pinch as my mouth opened. Did he really think I was that stupid? He wasn't the Lorren. The Lorren is a maze. The Lorren's made of gold. The Lorren kills people. What an ass. I folded my arms and cocked my head, allowing my annoyance to become visible. "You're not the Lorren. Nice try Valefar-boy, but I met the Lorren and he doesn't play this way. So who the hell are you?" I stared up at him with my arms folded over my chest.

"You're insane." He folded his arms and stared back down at me. I waited for more, but he didn't say anything else.

My face scrunched up as I'd had all I could take of him. "The hell with you, Lorren-boy. I seem to be totally screwed because of you. Not only did you not let me die, but you only half healed me, so I'm gonna die anyway—just slower. Thanks for the agony. Not to mention getting us totally lost inside the maze." I shook my head and started to walk away from him.

How could I get out of here? Effonating in and out was not possible. The only reason it worked before was because I appeared at the mouth of the tunnel. Once inside of it, the Lorren screwed with magic and bent it to its will. His laughter made me stop. I paused to look at him. His stance loosened. It was like he didn't know what to think of me, which was fine because I didn't care.

"You don't listen," he said exasperated. "My name is Lorren. I didn't say I was thee Lorren. And we aren't lost. I live here. I can take you back to where I found you and let you die alone, even though that's a dumbass idea."

I arched an eyebrow and walked towards him. He was taller than me. Everyone was taller than me. "I seem to be a dumbass girl. So tell me, Mr. Lorren, what would you do, if you were me?"

I regarded him suspiciously. If he was a Valefar, why didn't he drain me when he had the chance? It's what any creature down here would have done. Half of the demons where out trying to find me, so they could take my power for themselves. The other half wanted to capture me so they could hand me over to Kreturus. And one crazy-ass Valefar, named Eric, wanted to kill me so he could have fun watching me die. I shivered.

A tight smile spread across his lips. He didn't like me much either. "There are two things I'd do if I were you. First, I'd realize that there is no way to escape the prophecy. You are who you are. Deal with it. And two, I'd get my soul back, so we can get the rest of that poison out of you before it kills you, and this guy Collin gets all your power. Or is that what you wanted?"

My voice was small, "No, it isn't what I wanted." I looked up at him and paused for a second before sitting down on a ledge. I didn't get anything I wanted. Nothing ever turned out even remotely the way I'd hoped. Staring at the floor I said, "I wanted to stop the prophecy. I'd hoped to stop it… You were right. I'm stupid. I screwed up."

He stepped towards me, "And right now Collin, and every demon in Hell, is trying to find you. I bet you anything they don't know what would happen if you died right now. They think all your power would die with you. Collin doesn't know that your power would all be his, does he?"

I shrugged, feeling foolish. "I don't know what Collin knows or doesn't know anymore. Kreturus went into him. He acted like Collin, sounded like him, but there's no way I can ever know for sure."

Lorren's face fell. "So let me get this straight? You were trying to prevent the prophecy from occurring by killing yourself? So, you found the only thing that could destroy you—the Guardian's fang—and you scraped it across your chest hoping the poison would kill you?" I nodded, but that didn't wipe the shocked look from his face. His voice rose an octave when he asked, "What'd you think would happen when you died? That the prophecy would just be over and we'd all be like, oops, guess we got that one wrong?"

Anger flared inside of me. "Stop talking to me like I'm stupid. I didn't know. It's not like I got a handbook or even signed up for this shit. And I didn't mean to scrape my chest." My fingers delicately touched the scar beneath my neckline. "I aimed it directly at my heart…and missed."

I didn't think his eyes could go wider, but they did. "Oh my God! So what happened?"

"Collin stopped me. He hit the fang as I swung it toward my heart, but it was too late to stop it from cutting me." Collin looked so utterly devastated when I'd left him. As I was speaking, my voice went flat and all the steam in my comments deflated. I looked up at Lorren the Goth Valefar. "So. Tell me. Just say it. I can see it on your face. You're thinking something."

"I'm thinking you're damn lucky. Collin is either overpowering Kreturus, so that he could save your life. Or Kreturus doesn't realize that Collin has part of your soul. If he knew, that fang would have hit your heart. But, the old demon has to know that Collin has a soul.

Ancient evil that's as rancid as Kreturus can't tell them apart even if they are in the same body."

"So, Collin may still be Collin?" A flicker of hope fluttered within me, but I was afraid to let it. I knew what I'd seen, and it terrified me.

Lorren shrugged. "There's only one way to find out. Either way, you gotta go find him and get your soul back."

His words surprised me, "Why?"

He smiled at me like I was impossibly naïve. "I'm not gonna slap you in the head since you already had a really bad day. Let me spell it out—if you don't get your soul back, then you are going to die. The sapphire serum can't be drawn out of your wound entirely without it. I've isolated the poison so that it shouldn't continue spreading through your body at the same rate. I've crystalized it to slow it down. That will give you more time, but the sapphire serum will weaken you. If you don't get it out, you'll die. This fix is only temporary and I have no idea how long it'll last. And then, when you die, Kreturus will get all of your power, since you," he repressed a look of disgust, "sliced off a piece of your soul and shoved it in Collin. If you want to prevent the Prophecy- stay alive—and get your soul back."

Figures. I finally think of something that will work to prevent me from becoming this crazy girl in the prophecy and it totally screws me over. "Fine, I see your point. And no, I don't want to be the one who destroys everything. So, how do I get my soul back from him?"

Lorren smiled, "You are new. A demon kiss. How else?"

I shook my head. "I can't give him a demon kiss. I've kissed him before and it didn't take his soul."

"You mean your soul," Lorren answered, "And, yes, you can. A Valefar can choose to resist temptation and kiss someone without ripping their soul out. Most just don't."

Shocked, I asked, "What are you saying? That he could have taken the rest of my soul whenever he wanted?" The thought was horrifying. I thought we were even—that there was no way for him to do anything to hurt me. It was part of what made it easier for me to trust him before Kreturus jumped into him. Swallowing hard, I realized the rest of what Lorren was saying. "…And I could take his soul?"

"Yes, except it's your soul. Why do you keep saying his?"

"Because he has a soul. He's a Valefar with a fragment of soul too small to let him be anything else. He almost died a few months ago and I gave him a piece of my soul so he'd live. He has both our souls in his body. And I have a piece of his soul in mine."

Lorren staggered backwards. "Ivy! Are you insane? You made yourself a Valefar soul mate?"

I bristled, "Not on purpose. And shut up! You weren't there. You don't know what happened! It's not like I had much of a choice. It was watch him die from a Martis wound or save him. I saved him."

Lorren turned away from me as his eyebrows rose in his hairline. He rubbed his eyes hard and shook his head. When he turned back to me there was urgency in his eyes. "Answer this—do you want the prophecy to happen?"

Anger exploded from somewhere deep within me. "No! What are you, deaf? What do you think I keep telling you!" What the hell was wrong with him? I said it a thousand times, but he didn't seem to believe me.

"I'm sorry; it's just that you aren't what I thought you'd be." His gaze lingered on my face. He looked at me like he was trying to solve a puzzle, but was missing most of the pieces. I hated puzzles.

"Join the club. I'm not even what I expected at this point. I try so hard to do what's right and it gets all messed up anyway. Like this." I hesitated. I was telling this guy, a perfect stranger, how I felt. I didn't like bearing my soul to people I trusted, never mind Lorren. I snapped my mouth shut and when I spoke again, I changed directions. The past was the past. I couldn't change it. But what I would do next was still up in the air. My voice was less certain. I didn't like the idea of finding Collin and trying to give him a demon kiss. And after what Lorren told me, it sounded like Collin could turn around and suck out my soul while I tried to get his. "So what do I do? Give him a demon kiss and take back my soul?" A thought occurred to me, "How do I make sure I don't take his soul, too?"

"That's just it—you can't. There are no discriminating demon kisses. A demon kiss drains the soul, and you need all of yours back to keep Kreturus from stealing your powers. If you don't take your entire soul back from Collin, you'll die. Then Kreturus reigns and everything is a hell of a lot worse than if you became ruler of the Underworld." He shook his head and moved towards me with a plea on his face. "No, Ivy, listen to me. You have to find Collin and drain him."

"But... I gave him my soul so he'd live. If I take it away then Collin will die, won't he?" My mouth hung open. I couldn't believe I was having this conversation.

Lorren nodded. His voice was cold as he spoke with a smirk on his face, "Yes, he'll die. But he's a Valefar. Who cares?"

I bristled and shot back, "I do."

"Why?" he asked, perplexed. He unfolded his arms and waited for me to answer. I didn't know if I wanted to answer him. I didn't want to explain myself to

Lorren, but he seemed to know a lot more than I did. I needed help.

"Because I love him." My voice was a whisper.

CHAPTER FOUR

After Lorren worked on me, I felt different than before. The immense pain stopped as the poison was isolated and frozen in my chest. Lorren said the sapphire serum would remain in the wound unless I did something to aggravate it. I wasn't sure what type of action would cause it to leak out and into my bloodstream, but I knew that I didn't want to find out.

The pain inflicted by immortals and their objects far surpassed anything I experienced as a human. The agony compares to nothing. Their fondness of unfathomable pain made me wonder how anyone survived a life like this. As it was, I was still aching and felt weak from the ordeal. Valefar and Martis healed quickly and I began to wonder why it was taking so long to feel better. Ignoring the exhaustion, I continued to listen while Lorren berated me.

He made it rather transparent that he thought I was an idiot. He took it upon himself to explain over and over again why it would be bad to side with Kreturus or give him all my powers. Instead of trying to convince him that I knew that, I finally just let him sling his condescension at me and nodded. I didn't feel like defending myself anymore. I saw his points. He knew more than me. I made irreparable mistakes—that were huge. Yeah, check. I got it. But he continued talking to me while walking us deeper and deeper into the winding maze. I had no idea where we were. The golden vegetation was thick here. The sapphire floor gleamed beneath my feet. This appeared to be the densest part of the tomb.

My mind was reeling as I tried to figure out what to do. I followed Lorren, mainly because he seemed like he knew where he was going—and because I was safer in the maze than in the Underworld or up above where Shannon and the Martis waited to rip me to shreds.

Lorren walked in long strides in front of me. He was speaking sharply over his shoulder, and I'd finally had enough. "Maybe you know some things," I said, "but you don't know everything. You don't know what Collin did for me. Now show me the way out. I'm done following you around." I stood in front of him feeling defiant, weak and tiny. There was something grand about the boy-in-black that made me feel small. It didn't help that the remaining poison left a constant ache in my bones that wouldn't go away. I was so upset and he was agitating the hell out of me.

The corner of his mouth pulled up into a lopsided grin. I couldn't tell if he was smiling at me or laughing at me. Either way, it was patronizing. "No, you need to see this before you leave. You need to see the rest of the prophecy. And you need someone to clue you in before you screw us all over." He looked me over, assessing me. "You know, there are two types of people—ones who live their lives, and ones whose lives live them. You need to be the former, not the latter. And right now, you are letting your life live you. It's crushing you and completely out of control. You can't just let life happen, not if you want some say in what happens to you."

I sneered at him, folding my arms to my chest, "You think I don't try? Lorren, you don't know the first thing about me. Or what I've done to try and not be the girl in the prophecy." I've tried so hard to overcome it. I thought if I was a good person, then those things, the things they'd said about me couldn't come true. The Martis, and the months of whispers that I overheard, plagued me. I knew exactly what they thought I would become—but I refused. With every ounce of my being, I refused to become the low-life demon freak that they thought I already was.

He stopped suddenly, and turned, pointing at me, "And that right there…that's your problem. No matter what you do, you are that girl. It's how you become that girl that matters. You're missing the details. It's all in the details, Ivy." He turned from me and walked into a dead end. The walls were coated with golden flowers dripping in jewels. The ground gleamed bright blue with chunks of sapphires forming an ornate pattern in the floor. It looked beautiful, just like any other part of the Lorren.

Lorren reached his hand out and pushed his fingers through the golden flowers. The long ropes of flowers slid aside as if they were on a curtain rod. Lorren walked the length of the maze wall, pulling back sections of flowers revealing hidden paintings below. The paintings were large and secretly hung beneath the mounds of jeweled roses and lilies, undisturbed and unnoticed. Scanning the wall, I watched as Lorren revealed painting after painting. The alcove in which they hung was massive. I turned, following him to see each painting in the series reveal more vibrant colors. Arms folded, I watched waiting to see whatever it was he thought was so important, but after a minute I saw for myself—the painting from the church.

My heart raced in my chest as my arms fell to my sides. Walking towards it, I was sure that it was the painting I'd stolen. The same painting that Collin had taken when he threw himself down here in my place. It depicted me standing precariously on a tiny stone, barely holding onto the fingers of a boy. It still looked uncertain as to whether or not I was trying to pull him up or drop him. I stared at the painting with my mouth hanging open. Lorren stopped, as that was the last painting he revealed, and stood next to it.

I walked over to it slowly, asking, "Where did you get that?" The painting—the prophecy—had caused so much trouble. This was the one that the Martis had protected forever and now it was in Hell, in the Lorren with a Valefar. The more I gazed at it, the more confused I became. I didn't see the apocalypse. I didn't see the destruction that they spoke of. I saw a terrified girl and a boy about to fall out of her grip. Collin.

He snapped his fingers to get my attention, which infuriated me. I wasn't a dog. "Pay attention," Lorren snapped. "That isn't the only part of the prophecy that matters. The Martis guarded that old thing for years, but it's only part of what happens. The rest of these tell the story as well. No doubt you didn't realize there was more to this, right?"

I shrugged. "I knew there were more." Collin had mentioned other prophecy paintings. There had been thirteen in all, but I'd only seen the one. Lorren gestured for me to come over and look at the canvases. Dread crawled out of the pit of my stomach and climbed up my throat, as I walked closer to examine them. These held details that I didn't know about, details that I was fairly certain I didn't want to know. These were worse than my visions. I couldn't tell what my visions were doing or if they were real or not. But these paintings—the prophecies—they were iron clad. Whatever they said would happen, would happen.

I swallowed hard, stopping next to Lorren. He looked down at me. I gazed straight at the horror encased in paint in front of me. Golden eyes were the only trace of the boy I knew. The rest of his features were contorted with hatred. "Eric." My hand reached out to touch the ancient paint. Lorren watched me, but said nothing. The painting depicted Eric confronting me after he turned Valefar. It showed him pressing me against the massive stone with hatred. I was depicted meekly shying away from him with a sorrowful look on my face. There was no fear in my eyes. My stomach twisted as I looked at it. That painting had already happened. Eric was irate when he found me. He blamed me for his death. He was no longer the kind, caring boy I knew. He was a deranged Valefar intent on making me suffer a horrible death. That confrontation scared me so deeply that I still trembled remembering it. I quickly shoved my hands in my pockets so Lorren wouldn't see. The only reason Eric left me alone was because he wanted to kill Shannon first. She was the one who doused him with Brimstone. I was sure of it. And so was he.

Lorren watched me carefully. His arms folded as he touched his face, asking, "This already happened? Didn't it?" I nodded. Turning Eric into a Valefar was the worst mistake I've ever made. I closed my eyes and looked away from the canvas, and away from Lorren. A hand gently touched my shoulder, and I looked up at him. His green eyes looked down on me softly, "You did it, didn't you? You turned him Valefar."

Again, I nodded, too ashamed to speak at first. "I found him dying inside here, towards the end of the maze. I thought he wanted to tell me something, but he couldn't speak. His vocal cords were burned away by brimstone dust." I spoke in a soft monotone, staring blanking at the painting. "I thought he wanted me to turn him Valefar—so he could tell me. But, I misunderstood…" my voice trailed off. I didn't know what else to say. This was the first time I'd admitted my sin to anyone. I assumed he wouldn't care. Most Valefar didn't care about anything except themselves.

When I looked over at Lorren he had a stern look on his face. I thought he'd say something more about my demon kiss with Eric, but he didn't. He stepped forward towards the next painting in the series, and asked, "What about the rest of these?"

My heart sank. I didn't want to look at these. They showed a future that I was trapped in, but wanted no part of. Swallowing hard I stepped towards the next horror encased in paint. The first prophecy canvas I saw was happy compared to these. The rest of them looked like nightmares frozen in paint.

We moved back to a painting that we skipped. My hand floated up to my mouth, and I pressed my fingers to my lips as sorrow overwhelmed me. It was a painting of Eric covered in chains, sitting in a small chair— completely alone. Fierce loyalty burned in his defiant eyes as he refused to answer Julia's questions. Pressing my eyes together, I shook my head sadly and looked away.

Lorren watched my reaction to it and then said, "This has happened already as well, right?" I nodded. "Tell me what happened here. This was before the Martis was turned Valefar."

Nodding I said, "Yes, it was." I told Lorren about Eric's trial.

He looked at me in shock, "They condemned him to death?" His tone sounded incredulous, as if he couldn't believe it. "But that's not right." When I looked over at him, he was shaking his head with his brows knitted together.

I laughed bitterly, "Since when do Martis do what's right? Eric tried, and look where it got him. He was a dead man the moment he met me." I stared at the painting for a few more minutes until I couldn't look anymore. Remorse filled me. I wished he wasn't the Seeker, and then maybe things wouldn't have ended the way they did.

Lorren pulled me to the next painting, recapping what I told him. And we continued down the wall. He showed me the succession of prophecies and with every painting, the images got worse. Some of them depicted grotesque scenes—battles yet to happen. I was in every painting, prominent on every canvas. We stopped in front of a prophecy in the middle of the series, my breath caught in my throat. It depicted me in a flowing black ball gown with a jewel encrusted bodice. Corset strings laced it up tightly. I was in that room, the same room I saw myself in during a vision I had several months ago—a vision that ended with me realizing I was the demon queen. My eyes seemed different in the painting, vacant, hollow like I wasn't me anymore. These things would come to pass. The paintings didn't lie, but I couldn't see how they could possibly reveal the truth either.

I turned away, covering my mouth. "I can't look at these anymore." I felt bile rise up in my throat. What had I become? How did it happen? Some of these things had already come to pass. That's what made it so horrifying. This was real. It was true. These things would happen.

Lorren shook his head and shoved me towards the next painting, "No," he said fiercely, "You have to look. This is what happens." His fingers wrapped around my wrist as he pulled me to the next painting, and then the next. "Do you see? Have you noticed the one unifying element that is in every single prophecy?" His eyes were cold.

I pulled out of his grip, and turned to him. "I see. I see myself in every single one. I see that I look haunted and hurt." I pointed to one that showed me in battle, with the tips of my hair glowing like violet flames. "In that one I look fierce and certain. But in none of these is there a damn thing that says I wanted all of this to happen. Yeah, maybe I play a part, but so does Eric, Collin, Shannon, Al and every other person in any of these! It's not just me! The whole world doesn't go to Hell because of one shitty decision that I made!" I was yelling, and didn't realize it. "I'm sorry, but it's not a destiny that I wanted." I hung my head, as Lorren walked away from me.

He pointed to a painting, asking me more questions and folding his arms. He walked back to the painting of Eric's trial. "This part mattered, greatly. And the thing that acted as the catalyst wasn't only you.

There are several factors at play…" he glanced over at me. "How did he escape punishment? I assume that he wasn't turned into a Valefar in front of the Martis army."

"He wasn't," I answered, "I saved him."

Lorren looked surprised. "You saved him?" I explained what happened and how the Martis condemned Eric for helping me. "We'd saved each other several times over the past few months. And down here. It's just, that last time I tried to save him, well…I screwed up. He was dying and I couldn't understand him. I thought he wanted to live and that was the only way I knew…" my voice hung in the air and I'd stopped speaking mid-sentence.

"But…" he prompted.

But, I liked it, I thought. But, I enjoyed tasting his soul. The thoughts brushed the back of mind and were too horrifying to acknowledge. I shut my eyes and shook my head. "But nothing. It's my fault he's a Valefar." Looking at the rest of the paintings it was clear. I set this in motion. My decisions were causing a cascade of effects that I didn't anticipate. There was no way I could have possibly known. I swallowed hard. "So this is it. This is what causes the Apocalypse. Me."

He nodded. "You and some other factors, but mostly you. But it seems to be an accident, which is shocking. A girl ends the world by mistake."

Normally, I would have sneered at him. But he was right. I shrugged, "I thought I could change it. I thought the prophecy could bend and become what I made it."

"It doesn't work like that. The prophecy is set in stone. This stuff happens," he gestured towards the paintings. "And you're the key. Do you see anything in these? Does anything jump out at you?"

I was about to say no, but something did seem odd. I knew all the people in the paintings. In every painting Collin's face was obscured, but I knew it was him. One painting depicted Shannon swinging her silver sword like a warrior. That was the night we closed the portal on Long Island. I walked down the line looking at the paintings again, and instead of seeing my demise, I saw… something. Something with Collin and Eric. But what? I couldn't wrap my brain around it. Collin and Eric. I stared at the paintings and realized it seemed like a piece of the puzzle was missing. I counted and there were only twelve paintings. After a moment I paused and looked back at Lorren. "There's one missing."

He nodded. "There is. It's the last one in the series. We were missing the first until recently. It was tossed in here a few months ago. But it's that last painting that says what happens—who wins. If you win, you defeated Kreturus and take his power. That makes you

Demon Queen. If he wins, if he steals your power when you die, then…God help us."

I looked up at him. "You don't think that I'll turn evil by the time I kill Kreturus, if that is what happens? How could you think that?"

He looked at the painting and back at me. "Because. It's all over your face. You don't want to be this girl, and yet you are. She is you and you are her; and yet, you aren't the same—yet. "

I laughed, but it was completely hollow. What were the odds that I would find the only Valefar who knew where these paintings were located? Valefar knew a lot and the ones I'd met were older for the most part. And everybody seemed to know more than I did, but no one knew where the other paintings were. I was lucky I'd seen the one. And as far as the Martis were concerned, the other twelve paintings didn't exist any longer. I wondered why they thought that. While I was thinking about the odds of me stumbling on the one guy who knew where all but one of the prophecy paintings was, I decided it was luck. But, I was a little too lucky. I mean, what were the odds of that? And for that matter, what were the odds that he'd know how to heal me, too?

I turned to him and shook my head. I couldn't ask him directly why he knew all this stuff. That usually didn't go over well. So I asked the next best thing, "So tell me, because I can't figure it out. Why are you showing me this instead of sucking out my soul?"

Lorren laughed. He laughed out loud like it was the funniest thing he'd ever heard. "Suck out your soul. Why would I do that?" A huge smile spread across his lips as he wrapped his arms tightly around his middle and tried to contain his laughter. "You really think I'm a Valefar!"

My words sounded like I was offended, and I was. Lorren thought I was an idiot. A bumbling prophecy girl. I snapped at him, "Of course that's what I think! You're in Hell, you look like a human, and you're slightly insane. You might as well have Valefar stamped on your head!" He was still laughing softly and shaking his head.

I cocked my head and considered him for a moment. He didn't show any signs of being a Valefar. It was just a weird place for anyone but a Valefar to hang out. "Fine. But, then what are you?" Lorren folded his arms and looked down at me. His green eyes sparkled as the corners of his mouth twitched slightly. His smiles seemed condescending at first, but I couldn't really tell anymore. I wanted to kick him; he was irritating me so much. Instead I said, "You smile an awful lot for someone living in Hell."

He laughed again and replied, "I can't see the harm in telling you, although I don't think I've said this to too many people over my lifetime." I had no idea what he was about to say, but since it wasn't public information I was a little more eager to hear it. The expression on his face shifted. The smile smoothed out and his eyes were locked with mine. "Ivy, I'm an angel."

CHAPTER FIVE

Stunned, I stared at him with my mouth hanging open. "What?" I squeaked. I don't know what I expected him to say, but that wasn't it. "That's not possible! You're in Hell. Angels don't live here. I think the Lorren smacked you in the head one too many times." My lips twisted into an uncomfortable smile. Was this why he was so intimidating? There was something about him that was so overwhelming, but I couldn't put my finger on what it was. Now, looking at him—even with his confession—I still couldn't believe it.

Walking down the wall, he began to pull back the golden flowers that hid the prophecies, concealing them completely with golden vegetation one at a time. He spoke over his shoulder while he did it, "You're very astute," he teased. "No, most angels don't live here, but I do. Let's just say I'm a remnant of the old guard." There was a smirk on his face as he said those last words.

A chill ran through me, as my stomach lurched. The old guard? Some very scary angel had occupied parts of the Underworld after Kreturus was defeated nearly two thousand years ago. They were the twisted freaks who left the Guardian at the Pool of the Lost Souls, and set traps to keep the demons contained within their world and out of mine. They were merciless. Their traps were cruel, but extremely effective. Still stunned and increasingly weary of this boy, I managed to whisper, "So you're an angel named Lorren, huh?" He smiled, nodding. I watched him as he moved the golden vines in front of him, not really paying attention to what he was doing. My mind was spinning faster than I could think. If he was an angel, and was left here by the old guard, it was possible that he didn't just live in this hideous maze. Dread filled me as words flew out of my mouth before they fully formed in my mind, "You made the Lorren, didn't you? The angels left it here. It wasn't something that was made by demons. The Lorren was made by you." There was an accusatory tone to my voice. I hated this place.

The person who made it was one screwed up bastard. And yet, it was this guy—and he was an angel. Confusion contorted my face, although I tried to hide it.

He finished covering the last painting and turned back toward me. "Yeah," he laughed, "I'm an arrogant bastard, and after I finished with it, I named it after myself. Seemed like a good idea at the time. The Lorren was the strongest defense to hold back the demons. No one has passed through it and lived—except you." He flicked a glance at me and scoffed, "And I seriously wonder how that was possible."

I shirked off his jab and said, "That's why you can live here, and the magic of this place doesn't affect you? It's not because you defeated the Lorren, it's because you are Lorren." He nodded. I looked at him again, as if seeing him for the first time. He was an angel that was living inside a tomb. In Hell. I folded my arms and looked up at him, suspiciously. "So, did the angels kick you out, or what? Why are you down here?" Eric had told me that all the old guard pulled out. There weren't supposed to be any remaining angels down here anymore—hence the hideous traps.

Lorren shrugged and began walking back down the golden passages that we passed through before. I followed him, still wary, not knowing what to think or if I could believe him. It was so weird. Why would he stay here? I wanted to get out of this place as soon as possible. Everything from the cold, damp air to the eternal night made me feel twitchy, like I was trapped in a tomb. Why would anyone stay here by choice? Lorren walked with a confident stride, but his shoulders slumped forward a little bit like he thought he was too tall. I raced to keep up with him.

He'd been quiet; walking away from me quickly like my question pissed him off. "By choice," he shot me a sharp look. "And, I wasn't kicked out. I check on things once in a while. We noticed there was a lot more going on in these parts than there had been—portals being opened from the wrong side." He shot me a snide look, "Ya know, from up there," he gestured upward with his thumb, "and that's a bit unusual. Most people don't want to go into the Underworld. A few months ago a portal was opened somewhere near New York. And then another one was opened a few weeks ago near Rome." We entered the golden room where he drew most of the poison out of my chest. The silver rose that he used to heal me lay on the ledge where he left it. He picked it up before turning to me. Tipping the petals toward me, he said, "That was you. You were the one responsible for opening the portal to the Underworld. Both times." It didn't sound like a question, but it seemed like he was asking me. It seemed like he was leery of something, but he didn't give me any idea of what.

Hesitantly, I confessed, "I opened the catacomb in Rome, and I was there when they opened the portal in New York. But it wasn't me who opened it. It was the Valefar."

He walked toward me and stopped less than a foot from me. I could feel the heat pouring off of him like he was on fire. I tried to step back, but he took another step toward me. Why did everyone think they could intimidate me? I was short, but I wasn't powerless. Angel or not, I could fight back. Part of me wanted to scream at him to back off, but part of me wanted to know what he was afraid of. I could see it in his eyes. He was afraid. What types of things scared angels?

His voice was deep and came out in a whisper, "The Valefar couldn't have opened the portal without you. You have the key." His eyes burned into me as his gaze intensified. "One Valefar can pass through a portal without your key, but that wasn't what happened, was it? Demons tried to escape. Valefar went in. And Kreturus tried to come out. You tell me that you aren't helping him, and yet you're the one who opened the portals, you are the one who has the key, and you are the one who gave him part of your soul." He inched towards me as he was speaking, like he was scolding a child. His face was inches from mine. His eyes blazed with fury.

I bristled, "You don't know what you're talking about. You weren't there. I told you that I don't want this. If you had the means to break the prophecy and make it so that it didn't exist, I would tell you to do it right now—no matter what it cost me. You don't think that I feel guilty about everything that's happened? You don't think that I tried to stop it? When you found me, I was half dead. I gave up my life to end all of this! You're blind if you can't see that." Somehow my angry speech made me stretch to my tip toes, so I could scream in his face. Breathing hard, I noticed how angry he made me. I didn't care if he was an angel or not. I knew who I was, and what I wanted, but he had no clue.

There was silence. Neither of us said a word. I backed away from his face, but I didn't look away. Lorren ignored me for a moment and gazed at the wall. Finally, his eyes cut to me. "I believe you."

What an ass! My jaw dropped open in disbelief. He acted as if I needed his approval—as if I cared what he thought. When words finally formed a coherent thought, my voice was sharp, "I don't care what you believe." I pushed past him and into the labyrinth. "I'm leaving."

He called behind me, "I'm here to draw out the rest of the poison when you need me." I didn't turn around to acknowledge him. My hands clenched into fists at the thought, *If I needed him*. Shit! I totally needed him. If I didn't get the sapphire serum out of me, I'd make the prophecy come true that much faster.

And it'd be that much worse.

But, the part that bugged me most was that I didn't know how this all ended. That last prophecy was missing. There was no way to know if I could fix all my mistakes. There was no way to know if I died, and there was no way to know if Kreturus took all my powers and went on a rampage in my world and then wiped out the angel's realm. Lorren was an ass. I hated him. But, he was a key component in how things would end. And for some reason, he was helping me.

CHAPTER SIX

I wandered through the Lorren until I found the place where Eric died. The maze was much easier to navigate since it wasn't blasting me with mind-altering mist and tempting me with Collin's kisses. When I first stepped foot in the Lorren, I thought it was beautiful. I thought the golden flowers dripping with jewels were stunning. I couldn't take my eyes off of them. As soon as I realized what they truly were, I was horrified. How could Lorren sit in there and allow all those people to die in that place? I didn't understand how something that was supposed to be good, could tolerate injustice. Then I paused, realizing that maybe the people who were turned into flowers were given justice. Maybe they were supposed to be there. Either way, the golden tomb made me crave the inky sky and dank air of the Underworld. I couldn't wait to be out of the false warmth.

As soon as I stepped outside the golden walls, I'd be a sitting duck for demons, Valefar, and other evil things. I kicked the ground with my toes, sending loose bits of rock skittering at the mouth of the Lorren. What was I supposed to do now? Pressing my eyes closed tight, I fell to my knees. I blinked hard, fighting back tears. When I looked up there was a familiar set of eyes watching me from the cavern walls. Up high between jagged spikes of black rocks was the dragon.

I regarded him and nodded. He swooped off his perch and landed in front of me. Ignoring him, I went back to my thoughts, sitting right outside the Lorren. The beast lowered his massive body to the cavern floor, laid next to me, and curled up like a really big cat.

The dragon. Why was this thing following me? And whose was he? Kreturus'? I looked at the beast and asked, "Why are you following me? You already destroyed me when you took Collin and gave him to Kreturus. Go away." I rose, brushed the dirt off my shredded jeans and walked away from the beast. A few moments later, I felt a massive gust at my back and the dragon was gone.

The bond was pulling at me hard as I backtracked further the way I had come into the Underworld. I had to get out of this place. The longer I stayed down here, the worse things became. I needed to feel sunshine on my face and breathe fresh air. I wanted the warmth of the sun to seep into my skin and get rid of the chill that invaded me since I arrived. Although the shadows were no longer shrouding me, it was still damp and cold. I could have effonated from the Lorren to the catacombs so I could leave again, but I felt so weak. I didn't think I had enough power to keep my attention focused the way I needed to so that I wouldn't hurt myself. Effonating wiped me out when I felt fine. No, I needed to wait a little longer until I felt I could hold my focus perfectly. Until then, I'd move about on foot.

Walking through the Underworld alone sucked. It reminded me of everything I lost. My best friend stabbed me in the back. Shannon. I'd hoped she would have believed me. I'd hoped she would have been on my side. But she wasn't. And the sad part was that I had no idea when she had changed her mind. It sounded like she lived the past year thinking I was destined for Hell, but said nothing to me. It didn't make any sense. Why would she help me, then? But I couldn't get over the rage on her face, and the words she spoke cut into me in a way that wouldn't heal. Her words were painfully wedged there in my mind, forever.

I shivered when I wondered if Eric killed her. The hatred in his eyes was burning bright when he'd asked me where she'd gone. And while I want her to pay for what she did to us, I wanted to deal with her myself—so I lied. I told Eric that Shannon was in Rome, when I knew that she was really in New York. The misinformation would also keep Eric away from me longer. I seriously doubted he'd come after me again without destroying her first. And the new deranged Eric was terrifying. Hopefully Shannon realized he'd be hunting her and stay alive for a while. That way Eric wouldn't bother me and I'd have time to find her myself.

The dragon followed me as I walked. I could hear him in the distance or feel the soft wind brush my cheeks when he flew by overhead, unseen. For something so large, he moved silently. I wouldn't have noticed it before, but there were telling signs that the beast was near; like the sound of grackles that filled the air constantly —somewhere in the distance - but never too close. It was as if something was keeping them away from me. The same thing happened with the demons. None of them made a grab at me either. They were afraid of the dragon—that had to be it—because I was utterly vulnerable, weak, and completely lacking in ninja stealth. That beast was the pet of the ruler of the Underworld. No wonder they were all afraid of him.

As I was thinking about the enormous beast, he landed in front of me abruptly. I let out a shriek and clutched my chest. "What are you doing?"

The dragon looked at me, and then turned his head back toward the way we'd come. He repeated the movement several times before I realized what he wanted. It seemed like he was gesturing for me to go back. I was the kind of person who talked to dogs, so why not respond to a giant lizard—especially since he seemed intelligent? I could use all the help I could get- Kreturus' pet or not.

"Why would I go back? I have to get out of here. I have to talk to Al and decide what to do, and this is the way out. This is the way back to Al and sane people." I passed the dragon and continued on, but the beast lifted his huge paw and slapped it down in front of me. Startled, I jumped back, surprised. His paw made a loud thwack as his claws hit the stone ground and reverberated off the walls. "Cut it out!" I hissed. "Go away! Leave me alone."

The dragon shook his head and suddenly seemed way too lithe for his size. Panic made my heart race as the beast used his body to encircle me. His maw loomed right in front of my entire body. If he opened his mouth, he could snap me like a tooth pick. Standing perfectly still, I waited to see what he would do. He grunted softly and pushed my arm with his maw, careful to keep his lips closed so he wouldn't touch me with his razor sharp teeth. He repeated the movement and I found my feet moving towards his forearm.

"What are you doing?" I shook my head at him. I wasn't angry, just annoyed. Why this animal was following me was beyond me. And now he was herding me whether I liked it or not. He pushed me again with his maw, less gently this time, causing me to stumble. I grabbed hold of his hide to keep from falling, at which point he slid his muzzle under my butt and pushed me up to the depression between his shoulders. I rolled into the place between his shoulder blades, as he flapped down once. Then twice. And we rose into the inky sky.

I buried my face in his cold shimmering scales as the wind screeched past me. The dragon from my visions had forced me onto his back and kidnapped me. Terrified, I held on for my life, clinging to his rigid body. Every time he flapped his wings the depression that made my seat shifted. I dug my fingers around the side of a scale and held on. The wind whipped past us as we traveled a different direction than I had been coming from or going to. Within a matter of moments, the dragon landed as gracefully as a hippo, and I fell off his back. Anger and fear mingled too violently within me to say much. Instead, I just glared at him. The dragon rolled his eyes, and nodded his head towards something.

Agitated, I turned to see what he was gesturing at and felt my heart slide into my toes. There in the darkness I saw someone sitting on a large stone. Dread pooled within me as I recognized the curve of his back, and the slant of his shoulder. I knew who it was before stepping closer.

Collin.

CHAPTER SEVEN

The bond tightened with proximity to him. Damn dragon. I glanced sharply at the huge beast, angry at it for bringing me here. He was Kreturus' dragon for sure. Why else would he do this to me?

Hesitation, anger, and terror were mixing in my veins as I stood behind Collin. I knew he could sense me, and I knew he was the one who told the dragon to grab me. Part of me was elated that Collin was sitting there, perfect and alive—like before. But so much had changed since he held me in his arms. And now things were screwed up beyond repair.

Slowly, I shifted my foot forward. Collin kept his back to me, not seeming to realize I was there, which was odd since I sensed him as soon as the dragon tossed me off his back. I would have sensed Collin sooner, but I was kind of overwhelmed by that whole flying thing. Damn dragon. I glanced back to see where the beast was, but there was no sign of him. It was just me and Collin alone in the dimly lit cavern. The noise of grackles screeched in the distance, but the area around us was still. We were the only ones here.

As I approached him, I wondered when Collin would sense me. When would he turn around and try to convince me that he wasn't Kreturus? Would he be different and change the way Eric changed? I couldn't bear that thought. Collin's lightness, his playful nature, and his intensity were the things that drew me to him. His loyalty was the reason we were friends—that and he made me feel like I could survive whatever life threw at me. In a sea of storms, Collin had been my rock. But now…what was he? There was only one way to find out.

Collin didn't turn as I moved slowly toward him. Tension built in my muscles, and I wondered if I was going insane. Why was I approaching him? He didn't see me. I could have run off without him noticing, but something made me hesitate. I couldn't say exactly what it was; something about the angle of his downcast gaze or the slump of his shoulders. Whatever the reason, something was wrong. Somehow he failed to notice his own dragon. That seemed impossible. How could he not see something the size of a truck? All the while, the bond was doing weird things inside of me - stirring, pulling, calming - and he sat there like he didn't notice. Surely it was doing all those things to him too. Surely he could feel my thoughts only a few paces behind him, but he never turned around.

Silently, I stood behind him. His silken brown hair shone in the dim rusty light. My fingers reached out to touch his shoulder, but I hesitated. Right then Collin gasped, and turned so fast that I didn't see exactly what happened. It was as if his senses were delayed. He had to know I was there. My scent wasn't shrouded, the bond wasn't silent, and any normal person would have noticed a chick standing an inch behind him—but Collin didn't. He didn't notice me until my finger was nearly on his shoulder. When he rounded on me, he had no idea who I was. Recognition didn't flash before his eyes as he grabbed my arm and threw me into the wall. I shrieked and tumbled back against the rock, nearly losing my footing.

If someone threw me like that a year ago, I would have cracked a rib, cried, and fallen to the floor. But not now. I staggered and regained my footing before springing at him. Arms extended I launched myself at him and shoved him hard while screaming. I was angry, so angry. My emotions erupted out of my mouth in screams. "What the hell did you do that for? You had your beast drag me here, so you can attack me!" I shoved him again, but this time when my hands collided with his chest, Collin's fingers quickly wrapped around my wrists.

He jerked me toward him, and held me in his arms. I struggled to pull away, but stopped when I felt his confusion through the bond. Collin breathed in deeply, as if he couldn't catch my scent otherwise. "Ivy." It was like he just recognized me, but wasn't certain that it was really me. His eyes were strange, hazy like he was in a mental fog. Collin slowly pulled me into a hug, and pressed his cheek to the top of my head. When he released me, I staggered back in alarm. Something was definitely wrong. It was worse than before. Before he tried to convince me that Kreturus wasn't inside of him, and that I didn't see what I thought I saw. There was no way he would ever convince me of that. But now he wasn't acting like that any longer. I wasn't even sure if he knew where he was. He seemed so out of it.

Concern and suspicion mixed as I asked, "Collin? What happened?"

He shrugged. "Not sure. Everything is blurred. My memories are messed up." He looked at me, confused. "Some are like a dream—or a nightmare. You died. I saw you die in front of me. A fang from the Guardian slashed through your chest. I tried to reach you in time, but I didn't. You weren't yourself. You were screaming at me, and I couldn't save you." His eyes were glassy and his expression became increasingly vacant as he spoke, "It didn't matter what I did or what I said, you wouldn't let me near you. You were terrified of me." Collin's arms had folded tightly to his body. He didn't have his normal confident stance. He stood like a man shattered.

The need to comfort him consumed me. I wanted to wrap my arms around him and tell him it was all right, but I couldn't. His behavior was too suspicious. Was this a ploy? Was Kreturus controlling him or was this Collin speaking to me? There was no way to know. I should have turned around and walked away. I shouldn't have listened to his words. But I did. It was one of those times where I knew I was doing something wrong, something that would screw me later, but I did it anyway. Compassion is a bitch.

Swallowing hard, I pushed back my suspicion, and said, "Those things did happen. But I didn't die." I reached to touch his shoulder, but withdrew my hand at the last second.

He looked up at me with desperation in his eyes. The expression was haunted. "After everything I did, I lost her. I tried to save her. I tried to stop the prophecy. I tried to keep her safe. But, I lost her anyway. And in the end...I was the one who killed her." Glassy eyes overflowed with tears as he stared vacantly ahead. The pain in his voice was too great. Suddenly it didn't matter to me if he had an ancient demon inside of him, or not. He needed me. He was Collin, completely and utterly in that second. The emotions flowing through the bond revealed everything he said and more. He took the blame for my death. He thought he was the reason I'd died.

Without hesitation, I reached for him. My hand rested gently on his cheek, as I turned his face to look at me. "I'm right here. It's all right, Collin. I'm alive." But his expression didn't change. It was like he locked down his mind to not accept what his eyes were seeing. I took his hand in my mine and pressed his fingers to my heart. "See? My heart's still beating. I'm alive. You didn't kill me."

At first nothing changed. He stared at me with haunted horror, like I was an aberration of his mind messing with him. I kept my hand over his with my heart racing under his touch. His deep blue eyes were locked with mine, and I could see him slowly accepting what his senses were telling him—I was alive. Shock had buried him so deeply in grief that it took him a bit to dig his way out. I stood in front him, silently waiting for the pain to flow out of his eyes and recognition to return. When it did, fear collided with longing. We were so close, and in that lost state, he was himself. There was no way Kreturus would allow himself to be ruled by someone so broken. Very little was penetrating Collin's mind. But, now that he actually saw me and realized that I was all right, well, now what?

He blinked back tears and spoke so softly that I could barely hear him, "The fang sliced you. I saw it."

I shook my head, "But I didn't die. It wasn't your fault. And I healed." I slid my fingers along my neckline just above my hidden scar. "See there's nothing there." Okay, that was a lie. But, he didn't need to know that I was still dying right then. My tank top covered the scar and thin blue line of sapphire serum that was still poisoning me. I took his face between my palms, "I'm alive."

It was in that moment that he allowed hope to penetrate him, and he heard me. Sometimes when things seem too far gone, hope is a fool's dream. And when the human mind passes that point, there is no bringing it back. I flirted with the edge of that line for a year. It was Collin who kept me from falling over the edge. It was Collin who carried my grief with me. And now, I was the one calling him back from the edge. In that moment I didn't care about Hell, demons, or Kreturus. Collin was the only one that mattered. The bond flared to life and filled me with joy, relief, and thankfulness.

Collin's gaze intensified as he realized that I was still alive and in his arms. His fingers clasped the sides of my face, as he lowered his head and pressed his lips to mine, tasting me as if he couldn't believe I was really there. The kiss was soft and warm. My stomach stirred as I leaned into him. His arms wrapped around my waist and he pulled me closer. Heart pounding in my chest, I allowed the magic of the moment to overcome me. I didn't think about the things that I should have considered. I didn't think about Lorren telling me that a Valefar could give a demon kiss to anyone, at any time. I didn't think about stealing my soul back. I didn't think about Collin setting me up to steal the rest of the power locked within me. I didn't think at all. We were all there was, all that mattered.

Breathless, he pulled away. Questions were all over his face, "How'd you survive? I thought the sapphire serum killed you."

I hesitated, not knowing what to do. Confide in Collin or not? Could Kreturus hear me? Was he still inside of him? I didn't know. I didn't sense the demon, but it was possible he was hiding. It was possible that I couldn't sense him. And if Kreturus was still possessing Collin, then he could use the knowledge against me. He could make sure I never healed. He could end my life as soon as he realized that Collin had part of my soul in his body, and that if I died, he'd have all my power.

Looking up into Collin's face, I made my decision to lie. Besides wondering about Kreturus' whereabouts, there was another reason not to tell him the truth yet. Collin thought he caused my death, and he couldn't live with himself. It broke him. Finding him like this let me know that he had a severe weakness—he couldn't handle losing me. If I told him that I had been poisoned and that the poison was still inside of me— slowly killing me—Collin would do whatever I asked to save me, even give his own life. He'd done that before. I couldn't risk losing him again. Maybe it was selfish, but I couldn't do it.

So I lied. I shrugged, and looked away saying, "I must be immune. It hurt like hell, but it didn't kill me."

Collin pressed kisses to the side of my temples and pulled me into his arms again. When he released me, a look of hesitation came over him. "Why were you acting like you were afraid of me before?"

Swallowing hard, I said, "I was afraid of you. I thought you were Kreturus." His expression shifted wildly as I explained what happened, and how it looked as I watched. "What else would I think? It looked like he took possession of you. I was terrified."

His fingers played with the long curls by my face, "And what about now?" A slow smile spread across his lips.

My heart pounded in my chest. Should I lie or tell the truth? Why did my life feel like a free fall? It was like I was clutching at the air trying to stop the inevitable impact that was destined to come. I hedged, "You've always scared me, Collin." I smiled at him, and turned away shyly, talking over my shoulder. I could feel his eyes on my back. "You said things I didn't want to hear, called me back from the edge of insanity, and challenged me to live my life better than I was. You're everything I've ever wanted, and feared, all wrapped up together. Of course you terrify me." My arms wrapped around my waist. The confession made me shiver. It wasn't the answer he was looking for, but it was the truth. And the bond let him know it.

Thinking back to the first time I met Collin, I knew our lives would be intertwined; I just had no idea to what extent—turns out that it was much more than I would have ever dreamed.

CHAPTER EIGHT

Reckless was the word that described me best. I kept doing what I thought was right, even if it was incredibly reckless. I was flirting with disaster and I was a terrible tease. Walking with Collin, and being so close to him felt good. I didn't want it to end. I revealed my plans to sneak to the surface to speak with Al. Throwing messages into the wind didn't work too great for me. Although I tried, I didn't know if she ever go them, and there was no way for me to hear her in return. A trip to the surface was necessary. But, when Collin found out that I'd planned on using the portal at the Roman catacombs, he cautioned me against it.

"You can't go that way," he said shaking his head. "Not if the Martis knew you entered there. And you said they followed you guys down here." We'd been walking through the Underworld like it was normal. Hand in hand, we strolled past the jagged cliffs that tore through the cavern floor and stretched up into the inky sky and out of sight. His dragon was nearby, but didn't get closer. The beast's massive wings were hypnotic looking. They seemed impossibly thin to carry such a massive creature. When the dull red glow that illuminated the caverns lit the dragon's wings he looked terrifyingly beautiful. So, I did my best to ignore the beast or acknowledge him the same way I would a cat or some other normal creature that decided to stalk me. Collin didn't acknowledge the dragon, but then why would he, if it was his? I didn't really care that the dragon was there, and the creature did keep the demons and grackles away. Collin and I walked on in silence with the beast looming in the distance like a dark cloud.

Collin hadn't asked what happened to my friends yet. I told him that they'd come down here to help me, but I didn't mention what happened after that. As we traced the paths that I'd walked with Eric and Shannon, emotions began to bubble from deep within me. They were too strong to hide and I could tell that Collin could sense my dismay through the bond.

"Ivy," he started hesitantly, pushing his dark hair away from his eyes, "if you don't want to talk about it, we won't—but, what happened to them? Where are Shannon and Eric?"

We stopped walking suddenly, as I was unable to control a shudder. What happened to them? It was the question I was dreading. I wrapped my arms around my middle to chase away the chill that shook me, but it didn't help. Nothing could help. Nothing could change what happened on the way to rescue Collin. I lost both of them. Taking a deep breath, I looked up into his eyes. Collin's face was full of compassion. He knew something was very wrong. But he was right; I didn't want to talk about it. Staring into his eyes, I knew that I couldn't admit that I drained Eric's soul. And, I could barely talk about Shannon without spewing venom so thick that it made my throat hurt. No. I didn't want to talk about them at all. Blinking, I looked away from his gaze.

My voice was flat, concealing the tremors that were shaking me apart inside, "Shannon turned on me. She said that I was corrupt from the time Apryl died. She'd been pretending to be my friend since then. We fought. She tried to kill me. So, I sent her to the surface by shoving her through a black glass. And Eric..." I paused, swallowing hard. How was I supposed to admit to Collin that I turned someone into a Valefar? The one thing that Collin wanted the most was his soul. The thing he confessed to me from the very beginning was that he would do whatever it took to undo the Valefar curse. And here I was, adding people to the Valefar army of the damned. Collin was understanding, but I didn't think he would understand my actions.

Not this time.

To confess that I turned Eric would poison our relationship. Collin would never look at me the same way again. The last time Collin and I spoke of souls and demon kisses, I was terrified. And now? Now, I admitted the idea held some appeal. A demon kiss—the act itself was horrendous—but I was part Valefar and it called to me. And at some point during my time in the Underworld, I noticed that I didn't have to try to act Valefar anymore. I just was. I didn't have to flip off my Martis side and intentionally change to my Valefar side. Somehow they became equally accessible, anytime I needed that part of me.

Swallowing hard, I said the only thing that I could admit that wouldn't skew Collin's perception of me, "Eric's dead." That was all that I could admit. And it was true. The Eric I knew was dead. The new terrifying version was still around, but I was too ashamed to admit it. I tried to save him, and failed. The old Eric, the boy I knew, was dead.

Collin's fingers threaded through my hair as I looked up at him. He pushed back stray curls like he did when we were at school and I was upset about something. Now all those times seemed so trivial. I thought my world was falling apart then, and he acted the same. His steadfast nature gave me hope. Maybe I wouldn't become the monster that fate carved out for me. Maybe I could still be someone else.

A curl slipped between his fingers and brushed my face. "I'm sorry about Eric. I know you guys were friends." I nodded at him, but said nothing. When I didn't speak he asked, "So, Shannon the shrew is a full-blown Martis? And you shoved her through a black mirror?" I nodded again. His gaze bore into me. Those blue eyes were so intense that it was impossible to look away. My heart raced below my tattered shirt. It felt like he could see right through me. He smiled, "Sounds normal. For you. And what else? What aren't you telling me?"

My stomach twisted in knots at the question. Did the bond give me away? Could he really tell that I didn't tell him everything? I couldn't tell him what I did to Eric. I didn't want to admit it to myself yet, and Collin—I just couldn't tell him. I couldn't risk it.

Finally he saved me from my thoughts and asked, "The glass? You can conjure the Locoician Glass! That's incredible!"

Relieved that he didn't more about Eric, I asked, "What? You mean the mirror?" He grabbed my hands and pulled me to sit next to him on a boulder. There was no one else around; it was just us in the darkness. The dragon, wherever he went, was out of sight for the moment.

He smiled at me, "Of course! That mirror hasn't been seen for centuries. It's a wicked looking glass—literally. It's made of a black mirror and brimstone. And it's cursed. No one's seen it since the demon Locoicia was killed. It was hers. And you can call it! That's amazing! What did you do with it?"

I didn't know what he was talking about. Confusion lit my face, "I didn't do anything with it." The idea of calling an evil mirror sort of unnerved me. I didn't realize I'd called it, and I had no idea what it did. One day it just appeared. Al thought it was evil, but she wasn't certain of its origins. Apparently she was right. That nun was always right.

I shrugged, "It showed up and I shoved Shannon through it. I didn't know what it was. The first time I saw it was when I had a vision about you. The next time was when I pushed Shannon through. It spit her out at the church in New York, and then it disappeared again. I haven't seen it since."

Collin's face fell. "You pushed Shannon through the mirror?" He closed his eyes, blinking hard. "Oh wow. That's not good." He turned toward me, "Ivy, the mirror is enchanted. It amplifies people's characteristics—their evil characteristics. Locoicia was a demon princess who wanted an army of unstoppable warriors. She would shove her slaves through the mirror to amplify their abilities. It made her army undefeatable."

My jaw dropped. "Are you saying I just made Shannon undefeatable?" My shoulders slumped, as I looked up into the thick black sky, and ran my fingers through my hair while pulling hard. What were the odds of that? Why does this stuff happen to me? Shaking my head in disgust, I looked at him saying, "She's their Seeker—the Martis chosen to kill me." The last part came out as a laugh. I'd enabled her to hunt me down and kill me even faster, and all without knowing it. Awesome.

"Yeah," Collin said with a coy smile on his face, "in the future, don't shove your enemies through the mirror." His voice was light and teasing. I shot him a look that said I was about to freak out, but he cut off my tirade, taking my hands in his. "It doesn't matter. She's up there. You're down here. She can't get at you down here."

"But that's just it," I said springing up from my seat and pulling our hands apart. Collin remained seated and watched me pace. I spoke at an increasing volume with my hands flying, desperation filling my voice, "I can't stay down here Collin. I don't belong here. I want to go home. I need to talk to Al. There are things happening that I don't understand. I can ask you about the Valefar side of things, but I'm part Martis too and if that part dies…"my voice trailed off. I couldn't even begin to fathom what my life would be like if I allowed that to happen. "I don't want to lose that part of me. I can't become the Prophecy One. I have to do this. I have to sneak up there and find Al."

At one time I'd felt that I could have told Collin everything, but not now. Not when things were so precarious. It could lead to my undoing. And then I wasn't entirely certain of some things myself; like why was Lorren down here? How significant was it that he saved me—especially since there is an army of Martis trying to kill me? I stared at Collin's face wanting to say these things, but feeling like I couldn't. I hadn't told Collin about Lorren either. I didn't know what to think of that whole situation, and I wanted to discuss it with someone very much. But, revealing Lorren would also reveal my fatal wound. I couldn't say anything. Collin couldn't know.

I needed Al for these things. I pushed back the thoughts before the bond betrayed me. Right now I knew that my emotions were running wild and that my thoughts were so jumbled he couldn't get an un-garbled read on me. One thought penetrated all the others. It cut through the worry and fear, shooting straight to the top of my mind.

Please.

CHAPTER NINE

He sighed and through the bond I felt that this was against his better judgment. He thought I was safer down here. He took my hand, "I'll take you to her, but we can't use the portal you're headed towards. We have to use a different one. Shannon will gut you the second you walk through the tomb." I shivered, and was about to tell him that I didn't think she could have gotten back so quickly, but Collin cut me off. "Sorry, but you have to realize what you're dealing with. Shannon is going to be everything she was—times a hundred. If she was good at something before, now she is going to be unbelievably fantastic. And if her job is to kill you, then you have to avoid her. Take no chances. There are no more near-misses, not with her. If you see her again, you have to realize that one of you is not walking away alive. If you see her again, kill her before she kills you."

I nodded. This is what my life had come to. It made me feel sick inside that Shannon had turned on me. I didn't want to think about it. If I could live the rest of my life without seeing her again, that would be okay. But the odds of that happened weren't good. Even with the poison in my chest.

Collin pulled me to my feet, explaining, "Valefar leave the Underworld through various portals. Once you know where they are, you can effonate there, and then pass through them. The living and the dead aren't supposed to mingle, and that includes us. I mean, me…and the Valefar. The angels went to great lengths to keep us separated from your world. But there are a few doors they didn't seal, because they didn't know of them." He winked at me. I wondered if he would have told me the portals locations if he knew there was an angel hiding out in Hell. An angel who would seal the portals. All of them.

I asked, "So, Valefar get around down here by effonating and then passing through a portal? We can't just effonate directly in or out of Hell?" He nodded. "But once we go through the portal, Valefar can effonate through the Underworld, just like they do above? They can go anywhere?" He nodded again. That must be why I never saw Valefar walking around down here. They didn't have to. And it avoided unnecessary unpleasantness with demon birds, dragons, and psychotic Valefar if they effonated. "Then why don't we just effonate to a portal?"

He replied, "We can't. The only portal you've ever seen is the one you came through to get down here. It's not safe to use that one again, and you can get to the other locations because you've never seen them," he paused gazing at me. "Besides, I'm not letting you out of my sight."

I smiled at him. I wasn't sure what'd he do. I asked, "So, you'll come with me?"

His eyebrows pinched together and he gave me a look that made me know that he thought my question was strange. "Yes. Why wouldn't I?"

I shrugged. "Just wasn't sure because of the way things happened before." I wasn't sure if Collin knew that Kreturus had been in him or not. He never acknowledged that he was possessed, and during the time we were apart, well—it was possible that Kreturus left him. Or Kreturus could still be in there, but I couldn't sense the old demon. Even during that kiss, there was no trace of the ancient evil. It was just Collin and his icy hot kisses that I felt.

He turned me towards him, "Ivy, I'll do everything I can to protect you, but I have to tell you something.

Kreturus and I have a past. He's targeting me, and not just because of you. When we were in New York, I told you that I made a bargain with him—my soul for yours." Collin held my shoulders, but couldn't meet my eyes, "That was the deal. I told you that I'd do anything to escape my life as a Valefar. I wanted my soul back. Kreturus promised me I would have it. Since demons have a tendency to lie and not follow through on their promises, I demanded part of my soul before I began looking for you. Kreturus gave it to me."

I couldn't believe what Collin was telling me. Kreturus had given him part of his soul? That meant Valefar could be restored! That meant that I could save Apryl and undo the horrors I inflicted on Eric! Hope soared within me and deafened me to the solemn look on Collin's face. If I'd noticed his expression, I wouldn't have jacked myself up so high on hope, because as soon as he finished his story, I felt miserable.

"Ivy, he gave me a piece of my soul. He said it was a down payment—a glimpse of what I would get when I completed my task. Kreturus went the Pool of Lost Souls and called my soul out. He took a portion of it and infused it into my Valefar body. My soul and my body were reunited. But, it didn't work." Collin released my shoulders and tipped his head toward the ground. The toe of his shoe scraped against the loose dirt. "As soon as my soul was reunited with my body, it became rancid—like it didn't belong inside of me. When the Valefar killed me, I was a good man with a good soul. When Kreturus gave me back my soul, I was an evil man with an evil body. The good soul and the bad body couldn't fuse again, not without force. So that's what Kreturus did. He forced the soul to reattach to me, and in doing so, corrupted it. My soul had to become like me to live within me."

Collin laughed coldly, folding his arms tightly to his chest. "I thought I outsmarted Kreturus. I thought that piece of soul would free me from him, but it turns out he outsmarted me. Because it doesn't matter how pure my soul was before, there is no way it will merge with my body ever again - not after living the life of a Valefar. But when he forced it, he forced the evil from hundreds of lifetimes onto that tiny piece of soul. And no soul could bear that kind of abuse. That bit of soul wasn't enough to free me from being a Valefar. It wasn't enough to lift the curse that binds me to Kreturus." He looked haunted, revealing a memory filled with pain that he didn't want to relive. He bargained with Kreturus.

And lost.

I threw my arms around him and kissed his cheek. He wouldn't look me in the eye, so I placed my hands on his cheeks, and turned his face toward me. Looking him in the eyes I said, "It was still you who saved me. It was your soul, no matter how tiny, that saved me the night Jake tried to kill me."

The intensity of his stare worried me. He heard my words, but it wasn't enough. He shook his head, disagreeing with me. "It was also my rancid soul that made you what you are. Ivy I did this to you. I set this whole prophecy into motion. It wasn't you. It was me. I'm the one to blame, and it was all because I couldn't accept my fate and live the life I'd been handed." A violet ring formed around his blue eyes as he spoke. Rage stirred within him as he took on a vacant expression, no longer looking at me, but staring at nothing. Life as a Valefar was a horrible injustice and there was no way to change that.

I nodded, "You're preaching to the choir." His head snapped towards me and I swallowed hard. Whenever he was enraged, I put my soul at risk. He could snap and suck it out of me without another thought. And apparently, I could do the same to him. The idea ignited a hunger inside of me that had been dormant. It wasn't the bond, and it wasn't lust, although I had plenty of that. It was raw hunger, but the feeling didn't come from my stomach like I needed food. It came from somewhere else, deep within, and felt like I needed…I cut off the thought and jumped away from Collin before I could finish the horrifying conclusion. What if he saw that soul lust within me? My arms wrapped tightly around my middle as I paced. What was I becoming? Why was my Valefar side growing? It was becoming stronger and more demanding.

What's wrong? The thought brushed my mind as his hand touched my shoulder gently.

I turned toward him, forcing a fake smile onto my face. The ring of purple had faded from his eyes. "Nothing," I lied. "I just know exactly how you feel. I thought my life would be different. More... normal. Like right now, I thought I'd be at school, hanging around the theatre, and watching you rehearse, while I painted backdrops and tripped over cans of paint. I thought I'd gripe about sitting through bio and accidentally set the lab table on fire." I smiled faintly. "Eric, of course, would know exactly what to do and put it out. Shannon and I would ride bikes through the dirt paths at the park as fast as we could without slamming into a tree. My helmet wouldn't fit right because my hair's too big. And maybe at the end of the year, before you graduated and left, maybe you would have asked me to prom. Maybe we woulda danced. Maybe things would have been normal, just for one night." Until I voiced those words, I never realized how much I wanted those things. I wanted a normal life. I wanted the friends, the fun, and the memories that went with it. And most of all, I wanted Collin, and a chance life for us to be happy. A normal life would have been a date. A movie. Dinner, maybe. But not this. Not Valefar, demons, and this unrelenting wave of crap that crashed over me since the night Jake kissed me. "But there's no prom in my future."

Collin gently slid his hand into mine and weaved our fingers together. He smiled softly at me, blue eyes full of expression, "I would have asked you." He smirked. "Probably after teasing you like crazy, but there is no one that I would have rather gone with." He pulled me too him, and kissed the top of my head. "We were dealt a crappy hand, Ivy. The only joy in my life comes from knowing you. Come Hell or high water, we're in this together."

CHAPTER TEN

I couldn't relax around Collin anymore. I had hoped that I would, but it was impossible when Kreturus was unaccounted for. And without knowing his exact whereabouts, I was leery of Collin because he could still be possessed. Kreturus held powers that I wasn't aware of, and it was possible that he had hidden himself inside the one person I would do anything for. That damn demon was smart, and I couldn't see him vacating for no reason. So the question was, if he wasn't in Collin, where was he? What was more tempting than this brown-haired, blue-eyed boy who went to Hell for me?

I had no idea.

So I was stuck waiting, agonizing over my decisions and second guessing myself. Every time I opened my mouth, I had to hide my distrust and carefully evaluate what I was telling Collin so that I didn't accidentally feed Kreturus information that I didn't want him to have. It was becoming more and more difficult to be around Collin and talk to him about anything. And there was no way that he didn't notice my behavior, even though he didn't say anything about it.

Looking over at Collin, he caught my gaze and smiled at me expectantly, "What's on your mind?"

I looked away, quickly steering my thoughts to some other topic, so he couldn't sense how apprehensive I felt. He took my look as shyness, but it really wasn't. My attempts to cover my butt were shameful. I hated lying to him and couldn't wait for this to be over. Things could go back to normal as soon as Kreturus reared his head.

I asked, "Can you tell where other Valefar are?" Collin arched an eyebrow at me with a surprised look on his face. "I'm not asking if you're all telekinetic or something, but I was wondering what the other Valefar abilities were. You said you showed me the two that wouldn't hurt me. I was wondering what the other ones were." We stopped walking suddenly, and ducked around some stone that protruded from the ground like giant toothpicks.

Collin held his hand out, and I grabbed it as he lifted me over the last mess of boulders. There was caution in his voice, "Why are you asking?"

Uncertain of his question, I responded, "Because I'm half Valefar. What other powers do we have? I was wondering what else I could do?" His hand was in mine and we were trying to maneuver around the lack of path in this section of the Underworld. It was like a landslide covered what was left of an ancient path in stone and rubble. I kept sliding and losing my footing. Collin caught me most of the time. Once, I fell on my butt and shocked my tailbone. It still throbbed. I'd been thinking that healing would have been an awesome power. While Al said I had that ability, I didn't know how to harness it yet so that I could use it when I wanted. That made me wonder what other Valefar powers there were, and if I could use them. I explained this to Collin, but the only response I received was a blank expression on his face. The bond was useless this time, revealing nothing. Whatever he was thinking, he was hiding it from me.

I gently prodded him with my elbow after I gracefully fell over a mini mountain of sand and stones. I smiled at him, "What's the matter? You don't want to share?"

Turning swiftly, Collin rounded on me. His eyes were wide and his words were low and dangerous. "Never suggest anything like that ever again. Understand?" His nostrils flared like I'd enraged him, but I had no idea what I'd done.

Taking a step back, I put up my hands saying, "Sorry. I didn't think this was a touchy subject for you."

His mood sank further, "That's usually your problem—you don't think." Normally he would have said this kind of comment in jest, although I knew there was an element of truth to it. The truth is easier to listen to when it was dosed in sugar. This time he didn't do that and it stung.

I bristled and staggered over the last of the debris on the path we were following. Throwing my hair out of my face, I turned back to him. His face was pinched. The bond was tumultuous; it felt like I was being strangled. "That was low. But thanks for pointing that out. No, I don't always think things through. Sometimes things turn into life or death situations and there is no time to think. I just thought it would be nice to know what abilities were Valefar and which abilities were Martis, especially since I seem to be having those types of experiences more lately." I looked over my shoulder at him. He visibly deflated.

He reached for my shoulder and turned me toward him, "It's just... I can't risk losing you. There are a million different things you could do as a Valefar. Some are tiny things—little powers that eat away at you. There's a point of no return with Valefar magic, Ivy, and I don't want you to pass it. I don't even want you to know where it is. If you practice them, you risk losing your soul—you risk becoming fully Valefar. And once you taste Valefar powers, it's difficult to resist them, even when you know the cost." He looked away from me, as if remembering something. When he glanced back at me his eyes were wide as he pleaded with me, "Please don't go looking for trouble. If you accidentally use your Valefar powers that'll be better than if you knowingly called them. Please, promise me you'll only call shadows and effonate. Nothing else."

I took a deep breath. If I lied, he'd sense it, but I didn't want to promise anything like that. What if I needed to defend myself? Or him? If I knew more about my Valefar heritage, it would help. Even if I didn't use it. From the expression on his face, I could see that he totally disagreed. Not wanting to fight, I said, "I won't go looking for trouble."

He arched an eyebrow at me and gave me a faint smile. "And…?"

"And," I smiled up at him, "I promise." I just didn't say exactly what I promised.

CHAPTER ELEVEN

As we made our way to a portal, we crossed some difficult terrain. The Underworld was similar to the human world above in some ways. The creatures of the realm used paths to travel down there, and generally speaking, each kind of being kept to their own. They didn't wander around, but we did. That left us out in the open and vulnerable. On the way, we'd crossed through places where creatures attacked us. The grackles even followed us into other territories, hoping to peck my eyes out. As we continued towards the portal, Collin explained that the deeper you went into the Underworld, the more creatures there were. When we passed through the outskirts on the way in, we didn't see many demons, dragons, or the like. But now, I'd seen more evil creatures than I ever wanted. Before I went down there, I wasn't sure if I believed that there were truly evil beings—but now—let's just say that I had no more doubts.

When we were closer to the portal, we had a confrontation with some demons. I had no shadows to shroud my scent, and they noticed me when we passed too closely to them. Collin was careful to maneuver me around other beings so that they couldn't tell I was there, but this time, the demons took us by surprise. They were eager to make me their own. I didn't quite understand what that meant, and didn't ask for details. Collin and I fought them like we were born for this. Nightmarish creatures no longer scared me. I could battle them with my silver comb in hand and flaming purple hair. Back to back, we fought them off until there were none left.

Fighting demons no longer scared me. The things that truly terrified me now were limited to my own reflection, and the thought of losing the boy standing next to me. I couldn't bear to accept what I was becoming, but I knew I was changing. I wasn't the same girl as I was a year ago. I knew things now, and saw things, that had changed me. There was no going backwards. And, recently, it seemed that everything had a price—a price that was too steep for me to pay. I was in way over my head with no way out. Those things lurched to the front of my mind in a sickening suddenness, and I shoved them back just as quickly. I'd deal with it later.

I squeezed Collin's hand and looked over at him. He returned the squeeze and smiled at me. Collin made me more confident. It felt like I could manage whatever was thrown at me when he was nearby. It'd always been like that. The only difference was the things I was dealing with before paled in comparison to the demons and damnation stuff that was thrown at me now. One misstep and I'd lose my soul, and cost Collin his life. Collin saw my face falter and gave my hand a little squeeze again. I feigned a smile, but it didn't reach my eyes.

The closer we got to the portal, the more the butterflies in my stomach tried to eat me from the inside out. My nerves were relentless, and I wanted nothing more than for this part to be over. When we emerged from the portal, Shannon might be standing there. I was going to be forced to kill her. I was surprised at myself, realizing that I didn't want revenge. She totally screwed me. She made Eric think that I was the one who killed him. Technically, my demon kiss did kill him, but the girl who looked like me and doused him with Brimstone dust was the true murder.

And that was Shannon. Confident, carefree Shannon.

It was unbelievable. But when she spewed words of hatred at me outside the Lorren, I believed it. She changed. Shannon and I no longer saw eye to eye on anything. And up until this point, I thought I'd want to wring her scrawny neck. I thought nothing would give me more pleasure than gouging out her eyes with a piece of Brimstone. But now that the moment was here, now that I might have the opportunity—I was filled with dread. It felt like I swallowed glass and the shards were ripping through me. Collin made it very clear not to hesitate if she was there. I had to kill her first, or we would die—both of us. We had the element of surprise. She might know we'd escape through a catacomb, but she wouldn't know when or which one. If my previous best friend was there, it would be luck. And the way things usually go for me, it would have been my kind of luck too.

Collin had taken me to a different portal than the one we entered through. Shannon, Eric, and I went into the Underworld through the catacombs in Rome, but this time, when Collin and I emerged we were in the catacombs under Paris. Apparently the Valefar used the graves of the deceased to leave the Underworld. And most of the Valefar never returned to Hell. Collin was an exception; he threw himself into that pit portal last fall and fell into Hell, and directly into Kreturus' clutches. No, most creatures that made their way out of Hell didn't want to go back. And I couldn't blame them.

When we surfaced in the tombs, every muscle in my body relaxed. No one was there. No Martis. No Shannon. I smiled at Collin, grateful that we caught a break for once. When we made it out of the tombs without incident, the night air washed over me. I breathed it in greedily, as if I couldn't get enough. The air had such a different quality to it than the air in the Underworld, where it felt, tasted, and smelled of death, decay, and hopelessness. But the air up here wasn't like that. It smelled of hope.

And freedom.

After we were certain no one was around, I wrapped my arms around Collin and smiled up into his face. "Are you ready?"

"Since when do you ask?" he laughed pushing a curl behind my ear. I felt fine. The weakness seemed to fade from the time I left the Lorren and I was ready to take us out of this place.

Smiling up at him, I started the effonation. Heat licked through my stomach and climbed my throat the way it usually does. I fixated on Al and St. Bart's church in New York. This was the longest distance I'd ever tried to effonate two people. It was slightly insane but we both agreed that it was much safer to move around up here this way. I was public enemy number one and the Martis would kill me on sight. The best way to avoid them was to avoid being seen. As for the other Martis that were in the church, we'd have to deal with that when we got there.

If I'd known how the sapphire serum affected my abilities I wouldn't have tried to transport both of us. But, I wasn't aware of what crystalizing the poison had done to me, and now it was too late.

CHAPTER TWELVE

The sapphire serum turned to ice in my chest as we effonated. It seemed to swell and the normal pain of effonation was compounded. I screamed in silence and I clung to Collin. As the boiling blood coursed through my veins, I locked my fingers tightly around him. Losing him before we touched ground at St. Bart's would be disastrous. Collin told me that if I effonated incorrectly, I could peel the skin off my body. There were some things that sounded painful no matter how powerful you are. I didn't care to find out what splicing myself felt like, so I focused on Al and the church as fiercely as possible. My nails dug into Collin's back. I couldn't help it. He could tell something was wrong, but was unable to speak or help. Not until we arrived.

That particular effonation was hard to describe. When a Valefar effonates, everything becomes incredibly vivid—like it's a supersaturated version of its normal self. It doesn't matter if it's a person or a chair. It's just more. Then it feels like liquid flames are poured through your stomach. The burning fans out into every inch of you until you can't possibly stand it another second. There's no air, there's only burning pain and intense heat as your blood literally boils your body into mist. That was why the pain in my chest at the site of the poison was so much worse. The serum was cold and didn't resist the burn of effonation. I'd thought that if I aggravated the crystalized poison that it would melt, but the cold place turned grew and grew. My body was rigid as fire and ice fought to kill me from within. The roar of flames that flooded my ears increased and drowned out my cries. I'd aggravated the sapphire serum and it was no longer frozen in place in my chest. It shot out crystalized tendrils within me, making me feel like I was being stabbed by tiny swords from within. Then, the poison leaked out and melted into my blood. I could feel it happening and couldn't do anything to stop it.

Collin's eyes were wide and his arms pulled me tighter when he saw the look of panic on my face. We weren't there yet, but I couldn't bear it. Not for another second. I did the unthinkable and stopped focusing on the church. The result was instantaneous. My skin felt like liquid and began to peel away off my arms. Collin looked at me in horror, screaming for me to focus, but I couldn't. The shard of ice was growing and stabbing me so fiercely that I couldn't stand it. I could feel Collin trying to maintain his own effonation, as the heat surrounding him increased. But, it wasn't enough to help me.

Suddenly, we collided onto the dark brown floor. A voice was screaming, echoing in the silent hallways. Feet ran at us from every direction. Collin jumped to his feet, but I was unable to move. I rolled onto my side, curled into a ball, and clutched at my chest. Sections of my arms and legs had no flesh, but that wasn't what was causing the scream to pour out of my mouth. It was the poison. It was melting and I could feel the serum sliding back inside of me in a slow trickle. It was like being stabbed with the fang all over again. The seepage finally stopped as the serum turned to cold crystal again as the last of the effonation effects wore off. Tears streamed from the corners of my eyes. I was aware of people around me, but I didn't respond. I didn't care where we were or who was there. The agony finally surpassed my pain threshold and I passed out.

CHAPTER THIRTEEN

Voices spoke around me, but the words were muffled. It sounded like they were speaking underwater. When I finally made out what they were saying, I opened my eyes. A frizzy-haired old nun hovered over me, dabbing my head with a damp cloth.

"You don't do anything small, do you?" Al asked. She patted my head again, and I realized that I was covered in sweat. Moving slowly I felt the bandages on my arms. Scanning the room, I looked for Collin, but he wasn't there. Al answered before I could ask, "He's fine. You're the one who took the brunt of it. We bandaged you up. Collin went to go get something to heal those wounds, since I don't have a healer here right now."

Sadness stirred through the pain. Shannon was their healer. My voice rasped as I spoke, "Something went wrong." I tried to sit up. Al gently helped me. "The pain was much...more." My hand gently touched my chest where the agony from the sapphire serum was the greatest. It was then I realized that I was wearing a sweat shirt. Someone changed me while I was passed out. I looked at her wrinkled face. "You saw?" If she was the one who dressed my wounds and put this shirt on me, she would have seen the scar—and the streak of blue poison still imbedded in my skin.

She nodded solemnly. "Is that what I think it is?"

I nodded and explained what happened. "I thought it would end the prophecy. I thought stabbing myself with the Guardian's fang would fix everything. Turns out, I thought wrong. I couldn't have been more wrong." I hesitated. "Is anyone else here?"

Al shook her head. "These days everyone is running off trying to stop the prophecy from occurring. I'm just an old Seyer, sitting here, waiting to see what happens next. So you caught me alone. Tell me girl. I see someone patched you up, mostly." She sat on the couch next to me.

I told her what happened, leaving nothing out. I told her about the Lorren, my plans to die there, and the boy who was living inside the deadly maze. "It turns out that boy's name is Lorren. He made the Lorren. And he's not a boy, Al. He's an angel."

Al's skin turned ghostly white as her eyes widened. It took her a minute to close her gaping jaw and recompose herself. "Then we're in much worse shape than I thought." She shook her head and stood, walking away from me slowly. Her black dress swished the floor around her swollen ankles. "The angels would only show up for two reasons. One reason is because the demons are winning the war and the angels have been forced to make more Martis faster than normal. The other reason—the reason that seems more likely—is because the Martis aren't fulfilling their purpose any more. As a group, we've strayed from the old ways, Ivy." Al shook her head as a worry creased her brow. "Things aren't the way they once were. Martis once had glorious power. We did more than govern our own, heal, and see visions of what might be. We were holy— a group of people set apart from the rest of the world. The Martis were loyal, kind, and used the power granted by the angels to protect humanity and slay the Valefar. But, as time passed something changed and our angelic power receded, until we were left with next to nothing. " She wrung her hands as she spoke and turned back to me. "We have no place among angels anymore. Not with the Tribunal executing those who stand up and try to do what's right. I'd hoped our kind would change and recognize how far they'd strayed, but that night they condemned Eric… " She shook her head, unable to finish.

One thing that was remarkable about Al was that she always knew what to do, and it was always the right thing to do. But now, I could tell from the look in her eyes that she didn't know. She didn't know what was coming or what to do next.

Her voice was grave as she looked at me, "Seeing an angel so close to home can't be a good thing. Angels don't mess in our world. If they're coming back, then things are much worse than I feared."

I wanted to comfort her, but I knew she wouldn't have it. Facts were facts, she'd told me. When life was hard it just meant we had to work harder too. The nun sat next to me, as I looked to her and said, "But Al, the Martis are as screwed up as the Valefar. They haven't been fulfilling their purpose for a while. It's not like this just happened. Why would the angels come back now? What's so pivotal at this point in time that they'd interfere, especially if they usually have a hands-off policy?"

"Because it's time," Al said looking impossibly old and worn out. Her shoulders slumped as she stared off into space, not focusing on anything while she spoke. "Because you're here, and the prophecy is ready to play out." My mouth shot open, ready to contest her, but she put her wrinkled hand on my shoulder in a soothing touch that silenced me. Her silver eyes gazed at me as she smiled weakly. "The prophecy will happen, Ivy. You must know that by now. There's no question anymore. Whatever paths we may have tried to put you on didn't work. You'll become the Demon Queen. You'll reign in the Underworld. It's your fate. And it's time. That's why the angels are here, child. It's time."

A fury of emotions whipped through me. I wanted to deny it—the entire thing. I didn't want to be the Prophecy One, but I was. My stomach slid into my toes, as I asked, "You don't believe in me anymore?" I looked at my feet, too afraid to hear her words. She'd lost faith in me. It felt like there was no air.

Al grabbed my arm and said, "Of course I believe in you," she snapped back to life, and the worried expression slid off her face and was replaced with determination. "I know you'll do what's right. I know you, girl. You have a big heart, but sometimes things happen and there ain't no reason. It just happens. It's the kind of thing that makes sense later if we're lucky.

"There's another war coming, Ivy. The angels and demons will fight. And you'll be the victor—there's no doubt about that. Remember who you are girl. It's what will make you into who you need to be."

Barely able to speak, I replied, "But it's already all laid out. I know who I'll be. If that prophecy comes true, I'll become the vile evil monster that Shannon told me about." My throat tightened as I spoke, "I'll be trapped in Hell." I slumped forward, resting my face in my hands.

"No, girl. That's the part that's up for grabs." I looked up at her confused. "There are staples in the prophecy—things that don't change—but there are still parts that are up to you, even if you win the war—even if you become the Demon Queen."

Swallowing hard, I could barely process what she'd said. There was so much happening, so many things that I tried to avoid, but now they were all crashing together and forcing me to become the one thing I dreaded most—Demon Queen. I didn't know what that meant. How could I possibly be ruler of the Underworld and be a good person? Life doesn't work like that. The wicked are punished and get sent to Hell. My entire life, I tried to be good enough to go to Heaven—but now there was no chance. My destiny was the Underworld—that horrible dark cold place where evil reigns. Swallowing hard I looked over at Al.

She patted my back. "Drop your preconceptions of good and evil. Most of life is lived somewhere in the middle, Ivy. Martis were supposed to be truly good like the angels who made them, but look at Julia. Look what she's done. And Valefar are supposed to be inherently evil like the demons that made them, but look at Collin. There are strange days ahead of us. An old Martis, a Valefar, and the Prophecy One will work together. I've seen it. It's the strangest vision I've ever had." Her eyes dropped before she looked at me. "You can do this."

"You saw me? You saw the vision of what happens to me?" I asked.

She nodded. "I have. I'm proud of you, although I can't tell you why." She had a sad smile on her face. "Just know that I'll be proud of you."

I nodded, not knowing what else to say. My life was being slowly destroyed by angels and demons, and their servants. There was no ideal of normal anymore. Al was one of the only people I could trust. Her words gave me an anchor of hope that I would cling to as everything fell apart.

I didn't want to talk about the prophecy anymore. I didn't want to ask her how I would destroy the world or what would happen to everything. Instead, I skipped to the practical question that had been lingering in my mind, "So this Lorren guy; is he trouble?"

Al shrugged. "I don't know. If he wanted to do something with you, he could have. Obviously he thinks killing you is bad, and that is exactly what the Martis have set out to do. No doubt that no one realizes you gave part of your soul to someone else -

someone who's been possessed by Kreturus—although, I didn't detect anything different about him. Is he possessed now?"

"I don't know," I answered through gritted teeth. The pain from my wounds was still intense, but the need to tell Al what happened before Collin returned made me talk through it. "I tried to find out, but I can't tell—I can't tell from the bond or from touching him. I tried a kiss too, and there's no way for me to know." I hesitated to ask the question that was burning in my mind. I'd thought of it a thousand times since Lorren mentioned that Collin could still give me a demon kiss. "Do you think he'd do it? Do you think Collin would demon kiss me? Lorren seemed to think it was foolish for me to be around him. But, I thought that Collin could have taken my soul several times already, if that was what he wanted. But he hasn't. Al, I don't know what to do." I slumped forward wanting to hold my bandages tightly to make the pain stop. Cascades of curls fell over my shoulders, when I leaned forward.

Al swatted my hands away from my bandages. "You'll make it worse. Don't touch." She sighed, fussing at my bandages. "Ivy, there are moments in life that define us. They happen and it's in that moment that we know who we really are. Those times aren't the ones where you get hours to decide or even seconds to prepare—they happen in a snap—and just like that," she snapped, "you made your choice. And so far, I can't say that I've seen you choose wrong."

"Neither have I," Collin stood tall and handsome in the doorway. He walked over to us and kneeled in front me. He touched my cheek gently. "I have something to help heal your effonation wounds. It'll burn, but what else is new?" He smiled at me. In his fist was a tiny black stone. "It's coal. I can mix it with milk, and when it's poured over brimstone, and then onto your skin, it'll heal. Althea, is there somewhere I can mix this up?" Al directed him to the kitchen, and Al and I were alone again.

She asked quickly, "Does he know? The poison in your chest…does he know it's there and what it's doing to you?"

I shook my head. "I can't tell him. Lorren said the only way to fix it is to take my soul back, and I can't do that. It might kill him. Or…make him like Eric." A terrible hollowness moved through my stomach. I wanted to vomit. I didn't tell Al all the details of Eric's death, just that someone else killed him and I thought I could save him like I saved Collin, but that it didn't work. He turned Valefar and was totally crazy. Since I didn't know if Collin noticed, I asked her quietly, "Does he know? Did he see the scar?"

Al shook her head, "No, but you need to tell him. You try too hard to hide everything and fix it on your own, but this is one mistake that can't be undone without him. And eventually, he will find out—whether you tell him or not." She hastily changed the topic when Collin walked back through the door. Al was right. I had to tell him, but there were so many ways that conversation could go wrong.

Collin took a piece of brimstone from his pocket and tossed it in the pitcher of black sludge. After unwrapping my bandages, he poured the thick coal and milk slushy over my wounds. My flesh sizzled and hissed as the liquid came into contact with my body. I writhed, unable to brace myself for the pain. Slowly, and painfully, skin regrew. When he was done, it looked as if it never happened. Now, that was some of that Valefar magic that didn't look all that bad. He healed me with, but he wouldn't tell me about it. Maybe making tar-colored slushies wasn't considered a Valefar power?

Rubbing my arms gently, I said, "Thank you. I had no idea how to fix that." I smiled up at Collin.

He put the pitcher down and kissed my forehead. "I'm glad I was here to help you."

"Me too, but I gotta ask... Wasn't that kinda weird? Evil Valefars using wholesome milk in their witches brew?" I smirk pulled my lips into a smile. The pain was gone and I felt much better.

Collin laughed, pushing his hair out of his eyes. "It was hardly a brew. And even evil people like milk. I enjoy cookies, too."

Al cleared her throat, "You two are sitting ducks in here. If the Martis come back or anyone asks me what I did tonight, you two are going to have a world of trouble. Better be off now." She stood and walked toward the door. Collin and I rose and followed her down the dark hallways.

Before we left the building, she leaned in and whispered, "Remember, you decide who you are. Not no words, not no angel, not no one. And, Ivy, don't leave your pie to get burnt. Got it?"

I smiled and hugged her, assuring her that I would take care of my "pie." In this case, my pie was my massive secret—that I had sapphire serum poisoning me and that I'd die if I didn't get my soul back from him. That couldn't be hidden from Collin much longer anyway. And even if I didn't tell him, he'd eventually find out. What was the worst that could happen?

CHAPTER FOURTEEN

There weren't any safe places for us to go, and I wasn't able to effonate anywhere without burning my skin off. I wondered if that was the effect of transporting Collin as well, or if it was the consequences of having sapphire serum in my chest. Either way, I didn't want to find out. Weakness plagued me, making my movements slow and awkward. Collin asked me if I was all right, but I couldn't tell him what was wrong, so I put on a fake smile and nodded, then continued to chatter about nothing.

But, as we continued to walk east on foot it became obvious that it was going to be an insanely long walk. I'd seen several run down churches out east by the sod farms when we were at the old stone church months ago. I hoped to find a church that was still occupied to keep hungry Valefar away, and then we'd only have to worry about a Martis stumbling on us. Collin's fingers were threaded through mine and he swung our arms slightly before turning me toward him.

A soft smile spread across his lips before he said, "Why are we walking? Are you afraid of effonating yourself to bits again?" His fingers wrapped around some loose curls hanging over my shoulders. His piercing blue eyes searched my face, looking for an answer.

I shrugged, "Maybe." The corner of my mouth pulled into a crooked smile. I broke his gaze, not wanting him to sense the lie. "I know it's stupid, but I'd rather be outside with you and avoid some pain—for now anyway. I'm turning into a neurotic mess, constantly having my heart ripped out of my chest and enduring crazy amounts of pain." Biting my lower lip, I looked up at him, "Can we skip effonating for a while?"

Pulling me close, his arms wrapped around my waist and he buried his face in my curls. "Of course. I'm sorry I can't take both of us. I wish I could. I wish I could save you from all the things you've been through." He broke the hug and held my shoulders. "But, we can't walk to Montauk, or wherever you're taking us."

I knew he'd say that. We didn't have money for a cab, and besides—it wasn't smart for anyone to know where we'd gone. The area was crawling with Martis and Valefar. The odds of stumbling on one of them were pretty good. And since we couldn't be certain if any of the people surrounding us were human or not, it was best to keep to ourselves. "Collin, there's no other way to get there."

"Yes there is." He smiled, crossing the street with his arms behind his back. He gave a little skip as he turned and ran off into the darkness. In a matter of seconds I heard an engine purr, and a dark blue car pulled up next to me. The blackened window slid down to reveal Collin grinning, "Get in, beautiful."

My jaw was scraping against the ground. It was his car. The same car he drove me in before. But, how did it get here? Slowly I reached for the handle like I expected the metal machine in front of me to be a mirage. "Collin…how?" was I all I could manage to ask.

He laughed, "You're always the most impressed by the simplest things. It's not the big stuff that fazes you—it's a car." I slid into the seat and slammed the door as he pulled away and found the nearest road that would lead us to Route 25. Bobbing and weaving through traffic, I sat there dumbfounded. My fingers slid over the leather seats as I examined the interior.

Finally I asked, "Is this the same car? The one you kidnapped me in?" My gaze turned to him with my mouth hanging open.

He winked at me, "Evil Valefar magic. I can make a car anytime I want." I wasn't sure if he was playing with me or not.

"Did you steal this car? You didn't. This is the same one. It's the same one that you drove me out East in the first time, before you knew about my mark. How'd you do that? Can you conjure up anything? Can you call people?"

He looked over at me surprised by my barrage of questions. Shaking his head he said, "There are things that you'll want to learn how to do, but this isn't one of them." His voice was stern as his gaze focused on non-existent traffic out the windshield. "You have me. I can do it for you. That's all you need."

Why wouldn't he tell me? What was the big deal? While I didn't understand his apprehension, I could sense that this topic was no longer open to discussion. It was one of the many aspects of being a Valefar that I didn't understand. Everything about being a Valefar came at a price. I wondered what the price of the car was, but I didn't ask.

We drove the rest of the way to the church in silence.

CHAPTER FIFTEEN

The floorboard creaked under my foot. I made sure that the little chapel was still in use before we went inside. The sign said they meet on Sunday mornings with no indication that they would be here late at night on a Thursday, so we went inside. Collin and I waded through the darkness. He insisted that we find some place that provided cover, but some place that wouldn't trap us. That ruled out the basement, so we went up to the ancient attic. The floorboards were wide old planks that were covered in dust. The room was mostly empty with a few pieces of furniture covered in dusty white cloths. The roof pitched to a steep point, leaving us walking bent over to avoid clunking our heads on rafter beams.

I pulled a sheet off a piece of furniture, and tossed the cover to the floor. It had protected a rose colored chaise with a scrolling back from a lifetime of dust. I was so tired that I thought I'd fall asleep when I sat down. Some of the springs were weird in the bottom cushion and poked into my thigh. I scooted down and leaned against the backrest. Collin walked past me and checked out the rest of the space. It had multiple points of entry, which made it harder to guard, but it also made it easier to escape. I felt the chaise shift as Collin sat on the end by my feet. He was silent so long that I finally opened my eyes and looked at him. There was something in his stance that made me uneasy, but I couldn't put my finger on why.

He finally asked, "Why won't you tell me?"

Swallowing hard, I asked, "Tell you what?" I sat up. "I'm fine. We didn't have to stop here, but I'm not sure what to do. I didn't think you knew either. I thought it was better to hole up here for a few days, rather than backtrack into Hell again." A shiver ran through me. I never wanted to go back there.

Collin's gaze was soft and questioning. It was clear that I didn't answer his question, but he didn't press. I knew exactly what he was asking me; Why wouldn't I tell him what was wrong with me. Why was I hiding it from him? The look on his face said he realized this simple truth. The bond confirmed it. I squirmed as my stomach flip-flopped, but he'd already turned away from me. He could have used the bond to press into me. If he did, he would sense the pain and weariness that plagued me. He'd realize I was losing my strength.

He'd realize I was dying.

I leaned back into the chaise intending to only close my eyes for a moment. Slow breaths of night air filled my lungs, and before I knew what happened, I was dreaming. That was the second time that Collin saw me sleep. It was the second time I was completely vulnerable in his presence. Apparently I trusted him more than I realized.

And as much as I wished it weren't true, the sapphire serum had left me severely weakened. Sleep seemed to be the only thing that repaired my body. The visions that had overcome me and pulled me into sleep before weren't the same as the dreams that plagued me now. Everything changed when I was poisoned. As much as I wanted to deny it, sleep was a requirement. Although I could stay awake longer than humans, I grew weary if I didn't rest. That would make me vulnerable, but I didn't know how to deal with it yet.

After I had the serum in my chest there was another notable change—my visions were gone. I hadn't had a vision and I no longer knew if I could, or if I would ever have another. I wasn't sure if I needed them, and the thing that bothered me most was that it marked that I was changing. I was no longer the same Ivy Taylor that I was a year ago, or even a few days ago. The fang slicing across my chest had severely altered me. I no longer needed to focus on becoming a Valefar before using those powers. They just came to me when I wanted them. And it wasn't necessary to shift back to being a Martis—it just happened. Using my basic power became more intrinsic, and I didn't have to think so much about what they were and how to use them. I was aware that anger ignited my ultimate power—the power described in the prophecy—but I was still uncertain of what it could do. The poison made me slow down. Perhaps that was why I noticed these things. It was possible that they would have happened anyway, but I couldn't be certain.

Sunlight was shining on my face as I cracked my eyelids open. Breathing deeply, I stretched and blinked until my eyes focused. Sunshine flooded through the small windows at the front and back of the attic. It was morning. I never thought I'd see the sun again. Delight in such a small thing strung a smile across my face, but it faded when my gaze fell on Collin's stormy eyes. He was sitting in an old chair across from me. His fingers were tee-peed as he tapped each one, watching me.

A cold shiver rippled through me, as I pushed myself up. My senses were in overdrive as the bond transmitted discombobulated messages radiating from Collin's violent mind. It felt as if I'd awoken peacefully only to be cast head first into a raging sea. Emotions were flowing through the bond with such rage that it was crushing me. My breaths became jagged as my skin prickled. Everything inside of me was screaming to run, but my mind wasn't listening to my body. I sat in front of him, frozen with fear. The eyes that were usually full of vibrancy were rimmed in violet, and filling with red, as sheets of rage poured off of him. He said nothing, staring at me as he ticked off each finger.

When I finally found my voice I asked, "What's wrong?" Part of me wondered if the slew of emotions struggling within him had anything to do with Kreturus. Could a demon live in someone without me knowing it? I needed to find someone who knew more about these things. My only links to this kind of knowledge weren't available at the moment, so I had to improvise.

His jaw locked. It looked like he'd been sitting like that for hours. When he finally spoke, his voice was low and freakishly calm. "I'm trying, God knows how hard I'm trying to help you, but it never seems to matter because, no matter what I do, you somehow launch yourself right back into the damn prophecy." His hands dropped to his knees, and he looked up at the ceiling while pulling his fingers through his hair. He finally returned his exasperated gaze to me. Damn it. I did something stupid. This was Collin, not Kreturus. And he was a completely pissed off, angry Collin. I slid my tongue over the back of my teeth trying to think of what to say was say. I opened my mouth a few times to try to explain, but no words came to me. What did he want me to say? He finally broke the silence, as he leaned forward in his chair and asked, "Do you want to be the Prophecy One, Ivy?"

I visibly recoiled as my face contorted, "NO! How could you even ask me that?"

"You're kidding, right?" he laughed. "You don't tell me anything. I have no idea what you're doing, but no matter what, you keep throwing yourself back to becoming the demon queen. Maybe he was right. Maybe you wanted him all along and you were using me. Gah," he said as he ran his fingers through his hair and slouched back into the chair. The turmoil that was radiating off of him was massive. It suffocated me like a lead blanket and I wasn't even experiencing it firsthand.

CHAPTER SIXTEEN

Cautiously I asked, "He who? Who said I wanted to be demon queen? Who said I was using you?" That was ridiculous. Collin was my best friend, and more. I loved him. I'd do anything for him, which is why it was totally ridiculous that he would believe such a ludicrous accusation. As if I could like anyone else. Collin used to tease me about the guys I dated, but I never really dated any of them. They were the means to make myself feel better. As calloused as it sounded, I didn't like them—I didn't even know them. But Collin knew my past, which is why it was crazy for him to have believed whoever said that.

When he wouldn't answer me, I guessed. The bond shot an icy confirmation that I was right. "Kreturus. He told you that." I jumped off the chaise and slid onto my knees in front of him. Collin never made any indication of insecurity. He was the complete opposite, which is why this entire situation was unreal. Collin's emotions were stormy because he doubted himself. He doubted what he knew and who he was. It was like the pillars that made him were breaking apart. "Kreturus is a liar. Of course he'd tell you that I'd want him and his power; but I don't. I only want you." I reached for his hands, but he shot out of the chair before I could touch him.

"I don't believe you," he snapped. I flinched. The words stung. His eyes burned, as his gaze tore into me. "I've never lied to you, Ivy. And yet, here we are, and you can't tell me the truth."

Jumping to my feet I walked over to him. I wanted to blurt out that I'd told him the truth, but I didn't—I couldn't—and he knew it. Sorrow flooded through the bond and we just stared at each other. It felt like I didn't know him anymore, and he didn't know me. There was a sense of distance and loss flooding through us. It was laced with so much remorse that I couldn't stand it. Slowly, the red faded from his deep blue eyes as his anger receded.

I made a few false starts, but words utterly failed me. Pressing my lips together hard, I finally said, "I don't want to lie to you, but I don't know what else to do. You can't fix what I've broken. You can't save me from myself, Collin. And I've screwed up really bad this time."

The expression on his face remained hard and impassive. "Trust me with everything, or trust me with nothing. I can't live like this. I can't watch this happen to you." His words were stated calmly and rationally, but they hurt anyway. Revealing the truth would hurt him more. The poison in my chest was lethal. He'd blame himself. I knew he would. How was I supposed to explain this? How was I supposed to tell him I was mostly healed, but that it wasn't enough?

Swallowing hard, I didn't think. I just acted, feeling that it was right. Reaching for the edge of my sweatshirt, I pulled it over my head, revealing my pale skin and a black bra. Collin's lips parted as he watched me. Confusion lit his face, but he'd see it in a minute. He'd see I wasn't coming onto him. He'd see that I was showing him the secret I was hiding. The room was cold, and I fought back a shiver. I had to intentionally make my hands stay at my sides, so I shoved them in my pockets. My heart raced as he stood in front of me. Fear ran wild in my chest, making my heart race and my hands sweat. I was afraid of what he'd do when he saw the scar that stretched across my chest. He stepped slowly towards me, his eyes fixated on the line that marred my smooth skin. He raised his hand slowly and touched his finger to the scar between my breasts. The pale line disappeared behind my bra on my left breast, reappearing on the other side until it ended on my shoulder.

His fingers followed the scar across my chest, slowly tracing the curved line all the way to my shoulder. The sensation of Collin's skin touching mine didn't occur to me until he did it. I thought he'd look at the scar. I didn't expect him to touch me, but he did. Standing perfectly still, my heart pounded as Collin pressed his fingers slowly against my skin. His hands were so warm, and he was so close. The scent of his body was intoxicating and I did my best not to breathe in big greedy breaths, although I wanted to. When his fingers grazed across the top of my bra butterflies erupted tickling the ceiling of my stomach. Under normal circumstances, his touch made me crazy. It was a direct link to knowing exactly what I was thinking and feeling. The touch between us was always supercharged like it might erupt at any moment. But this was much more than I bargained for. Knees buckling, I could barely stand there and all thoughts vacated my mind, as soon as his skin touched mine.

Fighting through the haze that was fogging up my mind, I noticed his fingers had followed the scar to the end of its path. He looked up at me questioningly. I'd told him I was fine, but I wasn't. Right now, without seeing the blue poison under the bra, it looked like I was healed and the poison was gone. It looked like the scar was the only thing that remained, but I knew once he saw the bit of blue, he'd know the sapphire serum was still inside of me. I had to tell him.

Taking the bra strap between my fingers, I slid the fabric off my shoulder, and pulled the top edge of my bra down. The deep blue line contrasted brightly with my pale skin. Heart racing in my chest, I fought to control my hands as they started to shake. Collin's eyes were wide. His hand reached towards the poison with his fingers extended, but he hesitated leaving his hand hovering without touching the site of the serum. I watched his fingers as they slowly lowered and gently brushed the blue poison beneath my skin. Collin never looked up at me, and when he finally pulled his hand away, he was silent. Completely fixated, he stared at the long scar and the small spot of dark blue.

Finally he looked into my eyes. Until that moment, he was so lost in his own thoughts that he hadn't realized what was happening. He didn't notice the effect of the touch of his hand on me. I hadn't meant it to be sexual, but my heart was racing so fast, and I wanted nothing but his hands on me. His mouth opened slightly when I thought it, and I blushed in response. He could hear me even though I wasn't thinking clear thoughts. The emotions and desires that were flooding through me in a silent scream weren't a secret. He knew. As he parted his lips to speak, the sound of metal scraping metal snapped both of our heads to the staircase. Someone was downstairs opening the door. Fear shot through me, quickly replacing lust.

Collin thrust my shirt into my hands and said, "Go out the back. I'll meet you where we agreed. Go." He wasn't frantic, but Collin was frazzled.

I stuffed my arms into the shirt and took off out the back of the church. The building was surrounded by sod farms, so the nearest spot that provided any cover was a depression where the land was too rocky for the sod. Instead of trying to smooth the land, the farmer had left a small gulch. Running as fast as I could, I made it to the gulch and threw myself inside. It wasn't far from the building, but it was far enough that we wouldn't be seen once Collin arrived.

I slid down with my back to the church, breathing hard. What was I thinking before? A shiver ran down my spine, and I suppressed it, assuming it was emotional overflow. I wasn't a prude by any means, but I didn't think about being with Collin like that. The thought terrified me. Although I wanted him, the truth was that having someone see into every part of me was horrifying. I'd be able to not only hear his thoughts, as he heard mine, but feel what he felt. That alone was terrifying. A kiss put us into a frenzied state where I wasn't sure where I ended and he began. Our thoughts and feelings fused together in a simple kiss. I had no idea what sex would do. I put my hand to my chest, and took a deep breath as my heart slowed to a normal pace. Looking up into the sky, I decided that I'd have to think about it later. There was no time now, and I didn't want more problems right then. Why couldn't we just be normal? I pressed my eyes together hard, wishing that I was normal again, when a familiar voice sent ice through my veins. A cold hand clamped over my mouth before I could scream.

"Shhh," Eric breathed into my ear. "We wouldn't want lover boy over there to know I was the one who sent those people into the building, would we? I need to borrow you for a bit." He pressed his free hand against a sharp stone in the side of the wall. The rock ripped through his flesh, and red ribbons of blood flowed down his wrist. My heart was about to explode in my chest, and that was before he did anything to me. As soon as he grabbed my mouth, and locked my neck in his arms, I fought to get away. But it didn't matter how I moved or twisted—Eric had me in a death grip.

His warm breath brushed across my ear as he pulled me tightly against his body.

I stopped writhing for half a second as he spoke, "I'm taking my hand away. Don't scream."

As soon as his fingers were away from my mouth, I inhaled to belt out the loudest scream I could manage, but before I had the chance, he slapped his bloodied hand over it. His blood flowed into my mouth. Horrified, I tried to spit it out, but he held my mouth shut and forced my chin up until I swallowed. "You're so fucking predictable, Ivy." Those were the last words I heard before internal flames consumed us and we effonated without my permission.

CHAPTER SEVENTEEN

The same thing happened as before. Mid-effonation the poison turned to a shard of ice and felt as if it was cutting my skin away from my body by slowly leaking out acidic poison. A scream erupted from my lips, but the sound was only absorbed by the void. When we finally arrived wherever Eric took us, I fell face first onto the floor. Gasping for air, I curled into a ball cradling my wounds.

"Get up, Ivy. Effonating can't kill you. And I fully intend to take pleasure in that, so this little stint won't work." When I didn't move his swung his foot into my side. The pain from his kick shattered the pain from splicing my skin off during effonation for half a second.

My body uncurled and he could see the wounds covering my body. "What the hell?" He bent down to me, and moved me like a hurt baby. His touch was gentle, as he examined my arms and shoulders. This time the spliced skin was on my throat as well. "What is this?"

Through gritted teeth I told him, "From effonating. I can't." I stifled a scream as his fingers touched an open wound on my arm. He released me and I curled back into a ball with tears running down my cheeks.

He kneeled over me asking, "How do I fix it?"

Although I was in so much pain that everything was spinning, that question broke through the agony. I glanced at him. The expression on his face was odd. It was like he enjoyed watching me writhe, but that he needed me to stop for some reason. Taking advantage of his momentary compassion, I blurted out the things he needed. He raised an eyebrow at the milk, but did it anyway. When he drizzled the slop over me, it burned and hissed. Slowly, the pain subsided as my skin regrew. Lying on my back, I stared up at a ceiling and wondered where we were.

Then I looked at Eric, confused. "Why'd you heal me?" I asked sitting up, and he backed away from me.

The anger that lined his face returned. "You can't die by accident. When I kill you, you'll know. And that I want to watch for a long time. Not some shitty effonation wounds." He gestured toward me. He walked across the room and sat down. Slowly, I realized where we were; or at least in part. The carpet that I was laying on was musty and had one of those unidentifiable brown patterns on it. The single bed in the room had an equally heinous bedspread, which Eric sat on as he looked down at me. A sink and dingy mirror were at the back of the room. He'd taken me to a hotel room somewhere.

Eric terrified me like nothing else. Looking up at him, I asked, "What do you want?"

Folding his arms, he smirked, "That's the thanks I get for saving you? And after I was so kind and shared my blood, too." The corner of his mouth pulled into a crooked smile. I didn't want his words to affect me, but they did. Valefar blood was powerful, and he made me drink his. I had no idea what that would do, besides corrupt me further. He stood and walked behind me. I refused to turn around, even though his movements intimidated me. Suddenly he was next to me whispering in my ear, "That shouldn't have happened. Effontating both of us shouldn't have spliced your skin off... And you know why it did. Tell me."

Repressing the urge to run, I sat rigid. "You screwed up," I lied. "You lost focus. Effonating two people is hard and you weren't strong enough. It had nothing to do with me."

His fingers were around my forearm before I could blink. He threw me across the room like a ragdoll. My head hit the wall, as my back crashed against the headboard at a weird angle. My muscles flexed, wanting to fight back, but I was so weak from effonating that I couldn't. Eric was watching me. He leaned back against the nasty sink, staring.

He finally said, "You're weak. Why?"

I looked away from him trying to figure out how to get out of here. It was a room. I just had to get to the door. A bead of sweat rolled down my spine. I shoved my shaking hands into my pockets, so he couldn't tell how much he rattled me. "You fed me Valefar blood. What did you think would happen?" I stood and faced him, blank-faced.

Eric's eyes turned to slits, "I've fed others Valefar blood and took them with me, too. They arrived with their skin on. You did not." He straightened and walked slowly towards me. The pit of my stomach fell into my feet, as I swallowed hard trying to hide my fear. "No," he said, "something happened to you. Something happened after I left you in Hell. After you sent me looking for Shannon, without telling me what you did…and lying to me about where you sent her." His eyes were rimmed in red. His expression was dark, as the look in his eyes intensified. "But I found her. And now I have you, so we can find out what happened in the Lorren."

Eyes wide, I asked, "You have Shannon?" I looked around, but Eric laughed.

"Yes," he answered, "But she's not here. I wanted to talk to you first, and maybe drain your powers a little. Just so you can see what you're in for, but something's wrong with you." He stopped in front of me and leaned in, almost touching my face. His breath washed over me as he spoke, "Tell me or I'll find out the hard way."

I shoved him. The new Eric made me feel guilty as hell, but his constant intimidation irritated me. If he was going to kill me, just do it. Don't sit there and play first. The shove didn't knock him off balance, but it was enough for me to throw in a punch. It connected with his jaw in a loud crack. The sound reminded me of the Guardian's tooth shattering, and fear filled me. I couldn't kill Eric, not after I'd done this to him, but I had to get him away from me. The noise made me hesitate when I shouldn't have. His fist clipped my cheek and sent me flying. My back hit the bed so hard that all the air was knocked out of my lungs. Frantically trying to get up, I tried to catch my breath, but couldn't suck in air fast enough. Eric leapt on top of me, pinning me to the musty mattress so that I couldn't move. With a quick yank, I tried to pull out of his grip. He barely had me. I should have been able to do it, but I couldn't. Panting, I rested my head against the mattress and stopped struggling. I was too weak. His eyes raked my body, looking. His fingers brushed over every inch of me, feeling. I gasped as hands went places they shouldn't go, and tried to punch him again. But he wasn't interested in sleeping with me. He was looking for something—for the thing that was causing my weakness.

"Tell me Ivy, or this search is going to become much more invasive," he commanded. He grabbed my neckline with two hands and tore my shirt open down the front. I didn't have to say anything, because he saw it. Eric was smart when he was a Martis, and even more cunning as a Valefar.

Breathing hard, weakness consumed me. I needed to sleep. My eyes were heavy, but Eric was examining my scar like I was a piece of meat. His thumb pushed back the top of my bra and he held it there. His hands felt like lead, groping at me. I slapped him away, sitting up, "You found it," I gasped. "Someone else killed me first. I'm dying. You lost." Weakness overcame me as I fell back onto the bed and passed out.

CHAPTER EIGHTEEN

This time when I slept, strange dreams filled my mind, and this dream was very weird. I was lost. Someone was calling my name—Apryl or my mom— but I couldn't figure out exactly who it was. I just knew that I loved the person and that they weren't here anymore. Wandering in white mist, I walked on all the while hearing someone calling my name. The mist thickened until it felt like plaster pressing against me. The heaviness of it was crushing my chest, making it hard to breathe. I choked, pressing my hands to my throat, and crying out for help that didn't come. My body fell limp as I died, but my soul didn't leave my body. No, this time, I remained inside. I was there when the Martis found my body and burned it. I was there when the fires consumed my skin. When the flames licked my flesh from the outside and consumed my hair in greedy gulps. Finally, when I couldn't stand it another second, I shot up screaming and the dream dissipated. Sweat covered my entire body and my heart raced like it would explode.

Eric sat across from me, staring. With my hand on my chest, I slumped back against the headboard. I was still in my bra and jeans. Eric didn't care that I felt uncomfortable, so no new shirts were offered. When I pulled my hair out of my eyes, and wiped the sweat from my brow, I noticed that my strength had returned. Effonating drained me, but sleep restored my strength. I glanced at Eric wondering how long I'd slept. He stared back with an intense expression. Remaining slumped against the headboard, I feigned weakness. I'd have to kick his ass to get away, and surprising him would make it easier. My voice rasped, "What do you want?"

He unfolded his arms from his chest, and leaned forward. "I wanted to put you and Shannon together and watch what happens as you two try to kill each other, but this creates a flaw in my plan." Surely he wasn't serious? He stroked his chin, thinking. "But, you're too weak now, so she'll rip you to shreds. There's no way you could possibly win. Whatever you did to her in Hell has worked wonders for her fighting skills." He pushed off the sink and walked in front of me. "That might be fun to watch anyway, even knowing the outcome. I can hear your heart beating wildly, even now, and the look on your face is too much to resist."

Eyes wide, I looked up at him. I hadn't moved, thinking playing opossum was the best way to kick his ass. It would give me a leg-up that I needed to get past him. But the look on his face said he had other plans. Without warning, he lunged at me. His golden eyes pooled crimson as his lips smashed against mine. His lips locked with mine and I felt him surround the tiny bit of soul I had left. His Valefar hooks dug into me as the razor wire sensation pulled. I didn't want to use my strength to push him off of me, but I had no choice. Eric didn't bother to pin me, so my arms were free. That was such a foreign thought. Nice, kind, sweet Eric forgot to pin me. But that wasn't him anymore. He wasn't the boy with the ironed jeans and the white sneakers. He wasn't the soft spoken, gentle guy who laughed at me in biology. He was this. Before the memories ended, my fist collided with the side of Eric's face. He staggered backwards and fell to his knees and broke the kiss. Stunned, he sat for a moment looking up at me. The expression on his face wasn't right. The way he looked at me made a cold chill run down my spine, as I stood there panting with my arms outstretched, ready to run.

Eric didn't move. His expression didn't shift. The irises of his eyes remained lost in lust, pooled blood-red without a single speck of gold, but the expression was haunted and hollow—like he'd seen a ghost. Part of me hesitated. Something happened. Something that wasn't supposed to happen, but I had no idea what. Whatever it was, it stopped Eric in his tracks, but I couldn't hang around to see what happened. Hardly a second passed from the end of the kiss, but I'd waited too long already. Spinning on my heel, I took off, and risked effonating to the only place I knew I'd be safe— somewhere that had someone to heal my wounds.

CHAPTER NINETEEN

"You're taking too many chances with that boy." Al doted over me. I was back in my old room at the church. I moved in there with Al after my mother died last year. No one bothered looking for me here because I was never here. Add to that, it would be totally insane to try and hide amongst the Martis. But I was. It kept the Valefar away, so I only had to watch out for Martis. While others may have said I was crazy for going there, Martis were the lesser of two evils. I could handle them and Al could help me. I was sure she would.

I laid and stifled a yelp as Al poured left over coal-sludge over my wounds. I was glad she saved it. After Collin had made the last batch, she had him put the remaining contents into a Tupperware pitcher in the fridge. Collin had to take his brimstone with him, but he agreed with Al that there should be another person who could heal me, so he dusted the top of the mixture with brimstone dust. Al had a poisoned concoction sitting in the fridge at the church. On the side of the pitcher she scrawled NUN JUICE in big black letters. She poured it over me, careful not to spill any on herself. The brimstone in the mixture could have killed her, but she poured like she was handling Kool-Aid.

She continued scolding me for being stupid as my skin sizzled and painfully regrew. She waved a finger in my face, "He ain't Eric no more. He's something else, and if you can't accept that, I can't help you." I nodded, knowing she meant well. When Al found me, I had no skin on my forearms and throat...and I was half naked. The thought made my stomach twist. It didn't look good for Eric, but it wasn't like I was trying to protect him or something. That would be insane.

A goofy smile slid across my face as soon as the hissing subsided. My eyes were fixed on the pitcher and the black letters. "Nun juice?" I laughed.

She tilted the empty container and shrugged. With half a smirk she said, "Makes sure no one else touches it. Not that they would. This stuff smells putrid." I laughed lightly.

Al's smirk faded as she said, "Collin's been looking for you. I told him you'd come and that you were resting." My stomach twisted when she said his name.

"You talked to Collin?" I sat up frantic that she'd told him what happened and who I was with. I grabbed her wrist, not meaning to pull on her, but feeling utterly panicked, "Did you tell him Eric took me? Did you say I was with Eric?" My eyes were wide as I sucked in a gulp of air, ready to bounce out of bed to undo the damage. Oh my God! What was I going to say to Collin? How could I hide it now?

But before I could jump up, Al placed her hand over mine, and sat down next to me. "Why didn't you tell him? Don't you think he'd understand?"

I pulled my hand back and slid back against the headboard holding my head between my hands. "No, he won't understand. He thinks I'm this incredibly strong person," I looked up at Al, feeling utterly hopeless, "But I'm not. Eric was a mistake I can't undo. Collin's fought his entire life to get his soul back. When he finds out that I took Eric's away..."

"But the reason why you did it matters," Al replied. "It wasn't because you were doing something bad. It was because you were trying to save him. Ivy..."

Eyebrow arched, I gazed at her insane expression. "Al, there's no time for this. He won't forgive me." I lowered my head onto my knees, fighting back tears that wanted to stream down my face.

Al was quite for a moment, and then patted my knee. "I didn't tell him anything." My head shot up, surprised. "It ain't my place. I told him you effonated back from wherever you were and that you were in bad shape. I told him to come around in a little bit, knowing you need to rest some." A soft smile spread across my lips. Collin wouldn't be irate when I saw him. I wouldn't have to beg him to listen to me, so I could tell him what happened. He didn't know.

Al continued, "You're like a daughter to me, Ivy. I'd do anything to help you. What's mine is yours and all that. I think you already know that." She smiled at me. "The last time I had someone like that was Eric. He was my boy. I trained him and raised him right. He was one of the best Martis I'd ever seen. I was proud of him, Ivy—so proud. And I can't say he done wrong with what he did. If you didn't save him in the courtroom, I would have. Injustice is not tolerable." She folded her arms and shook her head, looking away from me. After taking a deep breath, she looked back up. "I knew that would be the last time I saw him. No matter where you took him, he couldn't come back. And I thought that'd be the last I saw of you as well. But here you are. Right in front of me again." She smiled sadly.

I didn't realize that Al didn't favor every Martis she took under her wing. It seemed like she was just as sweet to Shannon and the others, but maybe that wasn't it. Maybe she was accessible to all of them, but somehow Eric and I had claimed special places in her life. She looked at me like I was a child—her child. Thinking back, she did the same thing to Eric when he first introduced me to her. She beamed with pride and blatantly said he was her favorite. I thought she was a spooky old nun, but Eric knew better. He knew how amazing she was. Al patched him up after the Valefar killed Lydia, the girl he was going to spend the rest of his life with. No doubt Al sat with him and warned him of God-knows-what, while he was trying to recover from that nightmare. She transformed him into someone good and bled most of the hate from his heart. Eric had very little left by the time I'd met him, and I understood why he had it.

Some anger is difficult to release. Once, Eric told me that we were alike, and that must have been why the old nun put us together. In some ways we were. We lost more than we could bear, and we kept things buried too deep inside. I watched Al's face as I was thinking these things.

A question crossed my mind, one that I hadn't had the guts to ask before now, "Why don't you blame me for Eric's..." I closed my eyes not wanting to say it.

When I opened them again, I looked into her aged face and asked, "How could you still talk to me after what I did to him? How could you sit here and act like everything is fine? I'm a monster. I did the unthinkable." Before that night I had no idea how much Eric meant to her. He was her child and I killed him.

She smiled sadly at me, "How could I not? How could I cut you off for being who you are, and doing what you thought was right?"

"I killed him. No, I did worse than that," tears were streaking my cheeks as I spoke. Al's gray eyes met mine but held no judgment. I couldn't understand why. "It was the very worst thing I could have done to him."

She shook her head. "No, that was done a long time ago. And you know it. Stop this. You are what you are, Ivy. You did what you thought was right, did you not?" I nodded at her. "Then stop this. Accept that you made a mistake, and it cost Eric his life. Things like that happen to the best Martis, so it's expected to happen to you—even more so. You'll have to make decisions faster and harder. Sometimes things will work out. Sometimes the price of the mistake will seem to be more than you can bear," I hung my head, feeling like I was drowning in guilt, but she flicked my chin with her finger and I looked up at her.

She continued, "One mistake doesn't define a person—it takes a lifetime of actions to do that. You will not sit here and wallow in guilt over this anymore. Push past it. There are bigger things to deal with, and you need your wits about you. We need to get the poison from your chest before something happens. For us to do that, you need to let go of guilt you feel about Eric. You don't have the luxury of time, Ivy. Grieve for him later. I'm not telling you to forget him, or forget your mistake. We just don't have the time to process all of it now. "

I felt sheepish for a second and nodded, swallowing the lump in my throat. "Does this kill me, Al? I know you've seen it. I know you've seen how all of this ends..." My words hung in the air as she tilted her head, studying my face.

"No," she replied, "you overcome this. The poison does not kill you. But it doesn't end the way you think." She shook her head, looking away from me.

"Then tell me what you saw, so we can fix this," I said. I added, "And I know it couldn't have been giving Collin a demon kiss. I'd never do it. So what else is there, Al? Tell me what you saw in your vision?"

The old nun sat down and looked over at me. She seemed distraught. With her fingers laced together tightly, she said, "You find Satan's Stone. I saw it. That cursed rock does exist, even though most of us thought it was only a fable."

Skepticism washed over me as I arched my eyebrow at her. "I find a magic rock that belonged to Satan?" A smile pulled at the corners of my mouth. I tried not to laugh. I wanted to believe her, but it sounded impossible.

Al shook her head, "Believe me; I know what it sounds like. If visions didn't reveal the truth, I wouldn't have believed it either. The legend of Satan's Stone is a story that's so old that no one remembers it anymore. Some called it the Devil's Rock, while others called it Satan's Stone—either way, it's the same thing. And its power is real. Very real. You find it... And you're healed.

"The last time that rock was seen was during one of the early battles in the Angel Demon Wars. No one won that first battle. It was documented that the fighting just stopped when a young warrior held a stone up in the air. By now you know Martis document everything. The library at Rome is extensive, so I went looking for the document and found it. The section of text concerning the stone is marked as a translational error."

"And..." I promoted, wanting to know more.

Al hesitated. Her eyes were wide, but she quickly blinked her emotions away. Watching her closely, I noticed she hid the fear in her eyes as quickly as she could, but I'd already seen it. Whatever Satan's Stone was, it scared her. "And if it is a translation error, we can see for ourselves, because I know someone who has seen the original document—someone that you and I used to know as well; someone intelligent, cunning, and very resourceful; someone who left you half naked after he tried to give you a demon kiss."

"Damn it! Eric! Eric is the person I need to help me?" I couldn't believe it. I ran my fingers through my hair resisting the frantic urge to rip it all out. "He saw the war letters and knows about the Satan Stone?"

She nodded at me, "He never mentioned Satan's Stone to me, but I knew he must have seen that passage in the original letter. He came across it while he was hunting you over the years. He mentioned finding the original translation. He was excited about it at the time. He always got a kick out of stuff like that."

Springing out of bed, I grabbed a pair of jeans, asking Al questions as I got dressed, "So if Eric isn't Eric anymore, I'm screwed right? Or do you think if I went to his old apartment, the papers will still be there?" I paused, and looked up at her as I pulled on a boot. There was a surprised expression on her face, so I added, "He had a book, you know—a book with tons of writing in it, and pictures of stuff. He threw it in my face when he found out I had Valefar blood, and made me look at the pages. He said it was years and years of work.." Eager to know more about it, I sat next to her and asked, "Do you think he still has the letter? Do you think it's in that book?"

She nodded. "Maybe. He wrote that book over his life. In the early days, I'd see him scratching notes in it when he stayed with me. I haven't since it since. I didn't realize that he still kept it, but that would make sense. He'd keep record of things so he didn't forget over the years. If that's the same book, there'd be notes in it about everything and anything. Better go get it before someone else does. Do you know where it is?"

Pausing, I shook my head. "The last time I saw it was the night that Jake came through his window. Shannon snatched the book when we ran. There were Valefar everywhere. After that, we were separated and I didn't see what happened to the book. Do you think it's possible that it's still in his apartment?"

Al looked uncertain, "It's possible. Eric would want it hidden if it contained information like that. After the attack, I didn't think he went back, but I didn't see the book either. He didn't have it with him the night you two closed the portal at the old church and forced the demons back into the Underworld. After that, Julia banished him and I didn't see him around these parts again. There's a slim chance he hid the book in the same spot, until he could return and take it, but Ivy…" she shook her head at me, "the odds of it being there are slim. The Martis leaked to the landlord that Eric was killed in a horrific accident. All of his things were destroyed. The only way that book is still there is if Julia didn't take it, and it was well hidden."

Ice dripped down my spine. I turned to Al, "Would she take it? Really?" Before Al nodded, I knew that Julia would take the book. Of course she would. The Martis covered their tracks and would have removed any proof of his existence. They thought he was a traitor. I wondered if they had any idea what their actions resulted in. If they didn't condemn him to die, he wouldn't have followed me into the Underworld and become one of the most evil Valefar I'd ever seen.

But I couldn't think about that now. It'd have to wait until later, when this was over. After lacing up my other boot, I grabbed a sweater and yanked it over my head, and said to Al, "Then I need to hurry and hope to God it's not already gone. Here's to hoping Eric paid rent several months in advance." I kissed Al on the cheek and ducked out and into the night.

CHAPTER TWENTY

Collin was waiting for me outside the church, but when he came running up to me we didn't hug like a normal couple. When I ran out the doors and into the night, I saw him standing in the shadows. My stomach twisted. There were so many things to tell him. We ran toward each other and stopped, toe to toe. He seemed unsure of something, although I couldn't tell exactly what was bothering him without touching him. The expression on his face was torn between anger and guilt.

I brushed his hand gently with mine and said, "He ambushed us. It wasn't your fault."

"I should have stayed with you. It was my fault. When I realized a Valefar took you, it was too late. Tell me who it was. Who did this to you?" There was fury in his eyes. He'd realized that it wasn't just any Valefar who tricked him—it was someone very intelligent with skills that equaled his own. Al's silence hadn't bought me much time, but it did buy me enough that I knew what I had to do.

Swallowing hard, I looked up into his face. I couldn't keep lying to him. And if Eric was trying to make a grab for me, and Collin happened to see him, I didn't want Collin to be caught off guard. Plus, he'd know that I lied and it would tip him off that something was wrong. "It was Eric. He's a Valefar…"

"But how is that possible?" he asked shaking his head. "You said he died. Ivy, I didn't want to press you about it before, but you need to tell me what happened. This is bad. Eric was a powerful Martis. He was very skilled. He'll be a difficult adversary if he wants to attack you." His lips remained parted and he blinked at me as he tilted his head, "Why does he remember you?"

This was the part I was dreading. I felt the words on my lips. I was about to tell him that I did it—that Eric remembers me because I was the one who gave him the demon kiss. Courage fled at the sight of his blue eyes. I couldn't think about anything but losing him, about never hearing his voice or feeling his touch again.

Lies suddenly tumbled out of my mouth in an unstoppable wave, "I was there when Eric died. That's why he remembers me. He was covered in brimstone dust and left him to rot. By the time I found him, he was nearly dead. I tried to help him, but it was too late. There was a Valefar there, someone I didn't know. I thought he killed Eric. I tried to fight him off, and I did. But it was too late. Eric was dead..." my voice trailed off. Looking down, I wrapped my arms around my waist, and I pulled tightly, trying to hold my mouth shut so I wouldn't spew more lies. Why couldn't I just tell him that I was the Valefar who drained him? I kissed Eric.

Collin wrapped his arms around me. "Ivy, you've been through so much. I wish I was there to stop it. I'll never let anything like that happened to you again. I promise." He kissed the top of my head as I cringed inside. I was scum. I had to tell him, but I couldn't. When he released me, he asked, perplexed, "But then why is Eric hunting you?"

The question came fast and loose. It sucker punched me in the stomach and I felt my jaw flap open, but no words fell out. Why was Eric stalking me? Oh yeah, he thinks I tossed brimstone on him and then demon kissed him. I was the one who pulled the trigger on his immortal Martis life and turned him Valefar.

I squeaked before clearing my throat and saying, "Who's not hunting me?" That statement was true enough. The bond wouldn't register it as a lie. There were tons of immortals looking for me…and one angel waiting for me to attack Collin, drain his soul, and return with my soul intact. I cringed at the thought.

Collin reached for me, gently brushing his fingers against my cheek and brushed back a stray curl from my face. "I know. I know everyone is after you. We can do this Ivy, but you need to tell me things like this."

"I didn't know…" I started to say, but Collin cocked his head sensing the lie. I let out a rush of air, "Fine, I did know. But I didn't think he'd find me so fast. And I kind of hoped he'd remember me a little bit. Isn't he supposed to? My sister has memories of me." I'd told him about Apryl as we were walking out of the Underworld. I wanted to take her with us, but Collin said she was bound to the Pool of Lost Souls and there was nothing I could do to help her leave that horrid place. So we left without her. My throat constricted thinking about it. I pushed down the feelings before rage overtook me. I hated that she was trapped there.

"That's different. She remembers bits and pieces of you because it was put there to haunt her. It reminds her of the life she had—the joys of the life she lost when she was turned Valefar. I'm sorry Ivy, I know you don't like to talk about it, but they aren't the same anymore. They need their souls back to recover, but you already know that's not possible. Once a Valefar acts like a Valefar, there is no way for the soul to rejoin the body…there is no way for them to go back to who they were before it happened. I'm sorry." His words felt like rocks dropped on my chest, one at a time until I couldn't breathe.

Stepping away from him, I looked up at the sky. "So Eric didn't spare me because he remembered me?" I looked back at him. "That's what you're saying, right? That he knows I was there when he died and is going to kill me when he catches me?"

"Right," he replied, "he can't kill the Valefar who bound him—you already did. So he's coming after you, the only other person who was there. It's revenge. But, I don't understand why he didn't just kill you or why he used that kind of magic with you. It was risky."

Curiosity spurred within me. I realized that Eric used some weird kind of Valefar magic, but I was afraid to ask Collin about it since he didn't seem keen to talk about such things. I took the opportunity to ask him, "When Eric effonated, I had no choice but to go with him. How did he do that?"

Collin's gaze turned from mine, his eyes widened. "He didn't make you effonate next to him? It was his power that pulled you? Not his?" I shook my head. "Tell me everything he said and did when he found you." I told Collin about everything from Eric forcing me to swallow his blood, to his taunting words and how he used people to cause us to run out in different directions. When I was speaking, Collin pressed his fingers to his temples and closed his eyes. When I was done he asked, "Did you swallow? Did his blood go down your throat?" I nodded. Collin let out a rush of air like something heavy fell on his stomach. He turned away from me, pressing his fingers to his eyes.

"Collin, please tell me how he did that. I had no idea he could do any of those things. It caught me totally off guard." I walked up behind him, and gently touched his arm. He turned toward me. I looked up into his eyes and said, "I can't protect myself if I don't know what he can do."

Collin started to speak and stopped. His arms folded tightly to his chest as he tilted his head. His voice was cautious. "Valefar can intensify their magic if they use blood. There are things that can be done with their blood or their victim's blood." He paused, staring at me. "He was able to effonate with you because he made you swallow enough of his blood to take you with him. It only works once, but he could have forced you to do it again. The blood allows the same magic that the Valefar wields to be used on the victim. It's helpful when fighting immortals. Most of the Valefar have forgotten how to do what Eric did, which is making me wonder how he knew to do it." Collin looked to me for answers, but I didn't know. Eric didn't say much, besides that he managed to nab Shannon, too. He probably baited her out and caught her the same way. And I'd turned her into something that I wasn't certain of at this point. Shoving a Martis through an evil mirror would have some seriously weird side-effects.

Collin continued, "If he wanted to kill you, he could have done it before I got there. If he wanted to kidnap you, you wouldn't have escaped. He knows what he's doing, and you don't—which is why I've been trying to protect you." Collin shook his head, and laughed hollowly, "When I realized you effonated I thought the bastard was going to slaughter you after he toyed with you first."

I shook my head. "That's what I thought, but he healed me after he realized what effonating did to me." Collin's fingers wound around my curl with a thoughtful expression on his face before dropping it and shoving his hands in his pockets.

"That makes no sense whatsoever," was all he said about the matter. He was right about that. It didn't make any sense, even considering that Eric wanted to torture me and have fun watching me die. He still could have done that, and I was so weak that I couldn't fight back—but he didn't. Collin's sapphire eyes bore into me, waiting for me to reveal something more, but I didn't.

"I know. It really doesn't make sense. Al reminded me that he isn't Eric anymore." I shook my head, trying to shake off the guilt that crawled out of my stomach. Collin sensed it. He tilted his head, but I shoved those feeling back down to where they were hiding, and asked, "Have you ever heard of the Satan Stone?" He shook his head. "Al thought it could heal the poison in my chest." Collin went white as his jaw locked. I wanted to comfort him, and tell him it was going to be okay, but for all I knew—it wasn't.

"Apparently," I continued, "it's a forgotten Martis fable from a really long time ago. Al's one of the oldest living Martis and said she barely remembered stories about it. She said that Satan's Stone can give its owner power, so it can heal me." I didn't really believe the words coming out of my mouth. It was a rock. What could it do? But, I learned not to question immortal objects. After walking through the Lorren, nothing would surprise me. So Satan hid all his power in a rock—I'd seen weirder things. I looked over at Collin, "But no one remembers the fable, anymore. All the documents containing mention of it are gone—except one. Al said there is a letter from the first Angel Demon War documenting how it ended—someone held up a stone and the fighting stopped." Collin arched an eyebrow at me. "I know, right? Sounds weird. But that document is the only trace left of the legend of the Satan Stone. And I know where it is." I took a deep breath. "Someone else had heard about it too, while he was tracking me down for the Martis. Al said he had the letter…"

Collin shook his head in disbelief. "Eric? You're telling me that Eric's the only other person who could have helped us? And now he's…"

I finished for him, "A crazy-ass Valefar. Yeah. Sounds perfect." I explained to Collin that we needed to go to Eric's old apartment and steal his book. I only hoped that I could find it and that Eric's stuff was still there. Turns out I should have hoped for something else altogether.

CHAPTER TWENTY-ONE

Eric's apartment was in an old three story brick walk-up. We were listening at the door and didn't hear anyone when a neighbor came out. A short round woman folded her arms and glared at me from behind thick glasses. Her black hair was smoothed back into a ponytail where it frizzed into a massive puff. Her shirt was a size too small and rode right at the top of her jeans. Startled, I gasped like I was up to no good, but quickly explained that we knew Eric.

Sympathy instantly diminished her previous perception of us. "Oh, I'm so sorry for your loss." Her eyes shifted between us as she rubbed her palms together. "I can't image knowing someone who died like that."

Wide-eyed, I glanced at Collin. He nodded in agreement and laced his arm through mine. His thoughts brushed my mind, *Play along.*

"It was," he agreed, "Ivy's known Eric since they were children, and wanted to say goodbye."

The woman nodded, with her mouth hanging open in an O, before saying, "Oh, that's right. There was no burial, because the body..." she cut herself off before she said anything else. "Oh, dear-heart, I'm so sorry." She blinked back a tear and wrapped her arms around me in a bear hug. I stiffened and tried to wiggle out of it, before Collin mentally chastised me to be more mournful.

When she released me, Collin continued, "As you can imagine, it's very difficult to get closure when things end like that..."

I shot a thought at him; *Do you even know what you're talking about? What did the Martis tell her?*

But Collin ignored me and kept talking to the woman as if he knew, "I suggested taking her to his apartment one last time to see where he lived, but it seems that it's already been rented and we didn't want to intrude."

The woman had her hand over her heart and looked at me with huge weepy eyes. "Of course! I know the girl who moved in there, after his accident; in fact we're good friends. I suppose I could let you in, just for a minute. Tahlia isn't home. I'm sure she wouldn't mind." Collin nodded somberly and thanked her while she ran off to fetch the key.

I arched an eyebrow at Collin, "How do they think Eric died?"

Collin shrugged, "Beats me, but the Martis must have covered Eric's tracks well, because this woman didn't expect to see anyone. Asking to see the apartment was the best I could do. Do you think you can find the book quickly, if it's still there?"

"It's worth a try. I saw where he hid it. I just hope it's still there." There was a niche in the wall where Eric withdrew the book before he thrust it under my nose. Eric was irate that night. He said that I undid a lifetime of work. He didn't like me then. And he detested demon blood to the point that he didn't treat me the same way once he found out I was tainted. But, his actions were different than his words. He saved me. I saved him. It happened so many times that I was beginning to think that we were friends. Eric had changed after our descent into the Underworld. I pushed the memory away, as Collin's fingers laced through mine.

"Pretend you're sad." He squeezed my hand.

I squeezed back, "Don't have to."

CHAPTER TWENTY-TWO

The woman opened the door to Eric's old apartment. It looked so different. None of his stuff was there any more, not that I expected it to be, but it still jolted me. It was like the Eric I knew had been blotted from existence. Releasing Collin's hand, I wrapped my arms around my middle and walked over to the window. These windows shattered when Jake came crashing through one night and attacked us. I slashed Eric in the chest that night by accident. I thought I'd killed him, but he just laughed at me and saved me— even when he wasn't sure about me.

The large woman who'd let us into the apartment then excused herself for a moment to go water Tahlia's plants. She remained in the apartment, but wasn't watching very closely. I stared blankly as the memories plagued me. Collin touched my shoulder, instantly pulling me out of the memories and I flinched.

I looked back at him. "Sorry. It's just...I don't know. It's like this was the last piece of him, and now it's gone." I didn't expect to get so choked up, but I knew it wasn't the normal pangs of loss I was feeling. It was loss laced with guilt—soul-sucking guilt.

Collin refocused my attention on the matter at hand, "Where was it?" he whispered.

Shaking off the slew of emotions, I walked over to the wall where the book had been hidden right as Peggy bustled back into the bedroom. She spoke to Collin while I stood looking at the bookcase, and back to the window wondering what to do. I couldn't try to get the book with her watching me. She'd think I was stealing. Peggy didn't leave us alone again, and I didn't get the chance to see if the book was still in the wall. Eyes wide, I pleaded with Collin to do something, but he shook his head slightly and brushed my mind, Later.

Not understanding his intentions, he thanked Peggy and we left. When we were outside, I asked, "Why did we leave? I didn't get a chance to look."

Collin had his hand on the small of my back and was pressing me towards the alley. "There's something odd going on. I'm not sure what, but I felt like we had to leave. We'll go back later, and get it when Tahlia's asleep."

That was the first time I'd broken into someone's house. I didn't like it. My mind flashed pictures of a thin thirty-year-old with dark hair waking up screaming, and beating me senseless with a frying pan. Once I entered her house, it didn't matter how quiet I was, my pounding heart made me feel like an elephant trying to tip-toe through her dark home. Collin waited for me nearby, but he wouldn't tell me where. He was being secretive and wanted to keep it to himself. I didn't understand why he wanted to keep things secret from me. Okay, maybe I did understand. I had my own secrets after all.

Narrowly missing the black coffee table, I moved around in the dark with ease. Thank God for Martis vision. At least I could see. Too bad stealth wasn't one of my abilities too. You'd think it would be. There are enough clumsy people in the world that gracefulness should be a requirement of being turned immortal, but it wasn't. Lucky me.

I scolded myself to pay attention. My bare feet treaded across the carpet to the wall with the bookshelf and the hollowed out space hidden behind it. I didn't know how Eric had opened the hidden space. That was the only problem, and it wasn't like I could knock on it to listen for a hollow place in the bookcase to make sure I had the right spot. Sliding my fingers over the wooden shelf, I pressed it as hard as I could near the place Eric had extracted the book, but nothing happened. My fingers ran up and down the wood looking for any sign of an opening, but there was nothing. Shouldering my weight against the thing, I frantically pushed, but it didn't give. Maybe the Martis were already here, took the book, and filled it in? The bookcase was part of the wall, and it wasn't revealing any secret doors.

A creak drew my attention away from the wall. The sound came from the bedroom. I turned sharply and watched the door. With my heart pounding in my ears, I stood frozen, watching a light inside the room flick on. The desire to run overwhelmed me. The muscles in my legs were flinching, ready to take off. But I forced them to remain still, and wrapped my fingers around Apryl's necklace, gripping it as if my life depended on it. For a few short seconds, it felt like my heart would explode. All I could do was stand there and wait as the woman moved around in her room. When the light finally turned off, I realized I'd been holding my breath and released it. I unclamped the death grip on my necklace and noticed the peonies bit into my palm. The sharp edge of the white flower cut the padding on my index finger. The drop of blood blemished the tiny white flower and ran down into its petals. I tried to rub it off with my thumb, but I just smeared it over both flowers. Annoyed, I realized that I'd have to rinse it off later before the blood dried in the crevices.

I stopped fiddling with the necklace and ran my fingers along the bookcase, wanting nothing more than to be done with this and leave. But, the built-in wasn't showing any signs of being tampered with. There were no depressions, no sagging boards, nothing that appeared to be hollow—nothing. Pressing my eyes closed, I leaned back against the wall and looked up at the ceiling. With every ounce of my being, I longed to find the opening. If I could find the niche in the bookcase, I could get the book and figure out how to get the poison out of my chest. There would be another option to heal me and no reason for me to give Collin a demon kiss. It would never come to that. Hysteria was building up inside of me. I locked my jaw to keep from crying out in frustration, and turned back to the middle shelf and pressed on it. Just when I was about to give up, my pinky fell into the tiniest depression and caressed the spot just right.

Sudden elation washed over me, only to be replaced with horror. I'd found the hidden niche, but as the wood panel behind the bookcase slid opened, it screeched an ear-piercingly high shrill. The sound filled the apartment, flooding it with noise. Sliding my fingers into the slowly growing crack in the wall, I tried to grab the book as soon as the panel opened, but there wasn't enough room to shove my hand in and pull the book out. My nails scraped against the side and top of the hole in the wall, but no matter how hard I tried, I couldn't wedge my fingers in and pull out the fat book. Heart pounding, I wanted the panel to move faster, but it continued sliding at its leisurely pace unaware of the situation its loudness had created.

Within seconds of the screechy noise starting, I heard Tahlia's quick footfalls. The lights flicked on in her room, and the sound of feet walking toward me grew louder. I stared at the opening in the wall, now nearly all the way open. A brown aged leather binding was sitting in the niche snugly. Shoving my fingers around the panel, I pulled and tried to make it move faster, but it didn't affect it. It continued to slide slowly. Panic shot through me, and started pooling like ice in my stomach. My gaze shifted frantically between the book and Tahlia's door. A scream was building up inside of me, but I swallowed it back down.

I wouldn't get caught. I'd grab the book and effonate out of there. Collin would heal me. I just had to get my fingers around the book!

The familiar scrape of metal on metal came from her door, as the knob turned slowly. Tahlia's bedroom door opened slowly, as I pressed myself against the wall trying to shrink into it so she couldn't see me. I didn't want to hurt her, but she couldn't know we were here. There was nowhere to hide. As soon as her eyes adjusted, she'd see me!

The raven-haired woman scanned the room, looking for the source of the noise. When her eyes darted towards the wall, she was visibly startled and looked up at me in disbelief. Her mouth opened, as panic lit her eyes with fear and her voice came out in a scream. But the scream was cut short and muffled immediately after it started.

Collin clasped his hand over her mouth, and spoke softly in her ear, pulling her back into her room. He focused solely on Tahlia, not looking up at me. Tahlia didn't take her eyes off of me. The brown globes were wide with fear. Her skin glistened and she was shaking as Collin gently pulled her back through the door. Her gaze didn't falter from mine, and her eyes never stopped pleading. Guilt swam in my stomach, making me feel like I was going to vomit.

Suddenly, the shrill screech of the niche's panel sliding opening was gone. Swiveling my head, I looked at the hiding place and snatched the huge brown book. My fingers found the same spot on the panel and I closed the opening. When I looked back up, Collin and Tahlia were gone. I pressed Eric's book to my chest. It was so valuable. I needed it, and we had to get the book without anyone seeing us. My life depended on it.

Collin explained that if the Martis didn't get the book yet, that they would come at me that much harder when they found out I had it. Neither of us thought that was a good idea. The plan was to sneak in and take it before anyone realized what we'd done. Collin and I had both agreed that if we woke Tahlia up, that we couldn't let her go. But now that it actually happened, now that I screwed up and woke her, I couldn't do. Collin came with me to take care of anything that went wrong. And this was wrong. Heart racing, I ran back to her bedroom. I was surprised to see him speaking softly in her ear.

Tahlia was in a trance. She sat rigid on the edge of her bed with a vacant expression on her face. The terror on her face was gone. The pleading on her eyes was nonexistent.

Collin's voice was low as he whispered in her ear. "You're dreaming Tahlia. No one came into your house. No one was really here. It was all a dream. Sleep now. Sleep." The woman closed her eyes, leaned back into her pillows, and drifted off into sleep. Surprised, I wanted to ask how he did that, but he pulled at me to leave with him. Looking back over my shoulder, I noticed it—a small drop of scarlet on the corner of her mouth.

Blood.

CHAPTER TWENTY-THREE

"I thought you were going to kill her," I said. My voice sounded funny—like I'd been running and was completely out of breath.

Collin looked over at me and arched an eyebrow, "How would that not draw attention to us?" He laughed, "Mortals pay attention to death. Smart Valefar don't leave trails." I looked away from him and at the wooden walls. We were sitting on the floor of an old boathouse down by the docks, not far from Tahlia's house. Collin said he had come here frequently before he met me. This was his sanctuary. He led us into the old building that stank of salty sea air and mildew. There wasn't much going on at this time of night. It was quiet except for the sound of the water splashing into the dock.

Holding the book squarely on my lap, I looked up at him almost afraid to ask, "Then what'd you do to her?" He looked at me like that was a silly question, but I pressed, "I saw blood on the corner of her mouth. I know it was yours, Collin. Tell me what you did." The last sentence was more of a plea than a command. Valefar powers that involved blood scared me. They seemed to be the most heinous of their kind. I had no idea how true that thought was at the time.

Collin's eyes cut to me as if considering whether or not he should tell me. He finally let out a sigh and leaned back against the wall, and folded his hands behind his head. "I told you that I'd take care of it, and I did. Why does it matter?" He dropped his hands to his knees and looked straight at me, making my heart flutter under his intense gaze. "Why do you have to know?" He stared at me, and I felt that it was a warning. He wanted to hide this from me as much as I wanted to know.

Frustrated, I folded my legs and set the book down beside me. "Martis don't use their blood for anything, so this part makes no sense to me. I want to know what you did because...well, I expected you to kill her. I thought, maybe, you didn't...because of me. But then I saw the blood and knew that you still did do something bad, it was just something else." I paused for a moment and then looked away from him and up into the cobweb filled rafters overhead. "I just want to know what damage I caused by waking her up. I'm responsible for whatever happened to her." My gaze cut back toward Collin. "I have to know."

There was no sparkle in his eyes, no lightness on his lips shown by the smile he usually wore. He looked at me and nodded, as if agreeing that I should know. "Valefar blood is powerful. It's used in making another Valefar, as well as forcing things to take an unnatural turn. We're the living dead—a body with no soul. I'm the only one, as far as I know, that has any remnant of a soul, but even that wasn't enough to overcome what I am. But you, your blood is diluted and mixed with Martis blood. Maybe your mixture of good and evil blood cancels itself out. Maybe it doesn't. I don't know."

The look on his face became troubled, but the bond told me he was scared—very scared. I sensed his hesitation. "But," he continued, "the point is that Valefar blood is toxic to mortals. It either changes them to Valefar or it can be used to manipulate the natural order of things." He paused, not wanting to tell me what he did. Something brushed against the bond, and I felt him slam it back down, trying to hide it from me. I stared at him, horror growing within me, wondering what he'd done. "The blood made her sleep, and forget. I used it to erase us from her mind. But, Valefar blood is intrusive. The process will continue, routing backwards from today, until she forgets everything she knows. It will corrupt her body from the inside, destroying it in the process."

Eyes wide, I stared at him. My mouth was dry, and I couldn't swallow the knot that had grown to an enormous size in my throat. "So, you did kill her." My voice was a whisper. The fate Collin bestowed upon her was worse than I thought. He killed her anyway, but slowly. Oh my God! That was so much worse!

Collin didn't walk over and throw his arms around me and tell me it was okay. I would have punched him if he tried. Irate, I jumped up and walked outside to the dock. The salty sea air blew across my skin and sent my hair flying. Was this what my life came to? Murder? I killed that woman. If we'd snuck in when she wasn't home, our lives wouldn't have collided and she wouldn't be dying—forgetting everything and everyone she loved—while I was... While I was what? Anger surged through me as I smashed my fist into the dock. The wood cracked under my hand and splintered, sending shards flying in every direction. Some of the fragments scraped my cheek as they flew by, while other pieces of wood lodged themselves in my hand.

I sat down hard on the dock and began to pick the splinters out of my fist. Unable to use my left hand as well as my right, I couldn't get all the bits of wood out of my skin. The wind blew softly, and long strands of my hair lifted and gently balanced on the breeze. I stared. The tips of my hair glowed purple like dying embers of a once raging fire. Pushing the loose curls back, I thought that my eyes were probably ringed in violet, too.

I felt his eyes on my back before he said anything. "There was no other way around it."

I nodded. My voice was cold, "So it seems—at least when I'm involved."

"What is that supposed to mean?" he stood next to me, still cautious.

I looked up at him, "Did we really have to do that to her? I mean, so what if she saw us. So what if cops were looking for us? So what if the Martis are looking for us? So what if they know we have the book?" My gaze shifted down as my voice dropped, "Everyone else is looking for us anyway. What's the difference? The difference to us is minor, but the difference to her...We killed her, Collin. She just won't know who did it or why." My voice was cold, the bottom of my stomach was ice, and the resolve that was flowing through me was intensifying. Why did I do things because people told me to? When we spoke about it earlier, I dismissed the idea of accidentally waking her up. I only accepted Collin's plan because I knew it would never happen and I didn't want to fight. But now? Now, I regretted it horribly. I should have said something, did something. It didn't matter that she saw us. I ended her life, just like every other person who crossed my path.

Collin could sense my thoughts. He sat down next to me, careful not to touch me, allowing me to have some private thoughts and process my feelings without him seeing everything. He swallowed hard. "There can't be any witnesses. Too much is on the line. This is a war, Ivy. There are causalities." I looked over at him, shocked. "Don't look at me like that. Don't act like you didn't know how important it is to keep you hidden. If they find you, you die. We can't leave any trace of our whereabouts. It's bad enough that Eric's tracked you down. But if more people find you? You know what'll happen, Ivy. We can't evade an entire army looking for you. And what happens depends totally on which side finds you first. Kreturus isn't done with you, even if he appears to have left you alone for the moment. And the Martis will kill you and ask questions later. This isn't over. It's barely begun. I'm sorry I can't shelter you from this stuff. It's the way things are. This is war. You knew what had to happen back there. Mortals are born and die. That's their life. I gave her the least painful way out of this that I could think of. I did it for you. I knew you'd react like this, but it had to be done."

My head snapped towards him. My eyes were rimmed. I could feel it. The anger that felt dormant moments ago flamed into my chest, making me hot and increasingly furious. Collin recoiled slightly when I looked at him. Something came across the bond at the moment, but I was too upset to detect what it was. Later, I would have wished I had. "No. I'm not doing things like that anymore. I'm not killing people, Valefar, angels or demons, or Martis without being forced to!" I jumped to my feet, feeling the need to run to burn off the anger.

Collin jumped up next to me and grabbed my wrist. The look I gave him must have been horrible, but he didn't let go. "You can't go. If you run, the poison will only wear you out."

Un-contorting my face, I felt the tension building in my shoulders. Practically crying, I looked up into his eyes and said, "I can't live like this. I can't be the person responsible for this. Look at me, Collin!" I shook off his hold and pressed my hands to my chest. "Look at me! I'm becoming exactly what the prophecy said I'd be!"

His arms wrapped around me tightly, as he crushed me into his chest. His hands cradled the back of my head and forced me closer to him. I struggled, half wanting to pull away, and half wanting to punch him. Somewhere inside of me, I blamed Collin for what I was. I blamed everyone. Eric. Shannon. Even Al. But the truth was I am who I am because of no one but me. It was my fault that woman would die. It was my fault that I had to steal Eric's book. It was my fault Eric was a deranged Valefar and Shannon was—whatever she was. Tears streamed down my face silently, as I stopped struggling in his arms. The rich warm scent of Collin filled my head as I breathed. The strong pull of his arms made me feel safe, and the way life had been lately—I needed to feel safe for a little while—even if it was a total lie. Collin's arms dropped to my waist so he could look down at me, but I kept my face buried in his chest.

"We'll do things your way from now on. I'm so sorry that I upset you like this." He kissed the top of my head. "You're right. Everyone is after us anyway. We can do things your way next time, even if it seems risky to me. I won't make you do something like this again."

Looking up into his face, I felt my stomach clench. It was all I could do to nod, and break away from his hold. I turned my back to him, and looked out over the still water. The night sky stretched down and touched the bay's inky blackness somewhere too dark to see. It looked as if the bay stretched right up into the heavens—some place I would never go. Closing my eyes, I wrapped my arms around my middle. "Maybe you're right. Maybe one person shouldn't matter…but I can't do it."

Collin stood behind me, brushing my hair out of my face as he stood next to me. The ends of my hair were brown now. The anger that was burning within me had extinguished itself. "It's because you're you. You matter more to me, than anything else in this world. You see justice through the darkness. You changed my life in a way that I never even hoped for. You are the most courageous woman I've ever known." A smile pulled up the corners of his lips, "And you scare the shit out of me sometimes." I looked up at him and laughed one short laugh.

His hand lifted to my face, and gently brushed my cheek before drifting back into my curls. He wound the spirals around his fingers while gazing at me. "You're beautiful, Ivy Taylor…"

His eyes were locked on mine, as his lips parted slightly. Lowering his head slowly, he meant to kiss me. The thought brushed the front of his mind, so gently that I could tell it was all he wanted. When Collin's lips touched mine, I felt his warm breath slide across my mouth. The butterflies that were tickling the top of my stomach went wild, and shot into a thousand pieces inside of me. His kiss was all consuming. It made me forget everything and feel everything at the same time.

The muscles in my chest tightened as he pressed his lips harder against mine. Icy hot sparks shot through me, leaving me feeling vulnerable and blissful at the same time. It was the dichotomy of the kiss that was intoxicating. It was a kiss that could kill, and it was a kiss that showed Collin could love someone like me.

CHAPTER TWENTY-FOUR

When we cracked open Eric's book, I never expected to find what was inside. Last time I'd seen it, I thought I recognized some of it even though I remembered some of the writing was weird. But now looking at it—I had no idea why I thought we'd be able to read it. Letters from an ancient language were scrawled across page after page of detailed notes. Collin was as perplexed as I was.

"The letters aren't even going in the one direction," I said, pushing my hair out of my face and wrapping it with a rubber band. When I leaned over the book again, I shook my head. We'd returned to the boathouse to examine the pages before anything else happened. When we opened it, I thought the book would be in English, but it wasn't. There were odd squiggles and they covered every inch of every page. I shook my head, looking up at Collin, "Do you recognize any of it?"

His mouth was hanging open slightly, as his finger dragged across the page. He'd been doing this for the better part of an hour, not saying much. He shook his head, "No. This is like Greek—they are Greek characters—well, for the most part. But, periodically there is something else thrown in. And it isn't written left to right. I tried right to left like some languages, and up to down like others, but there is no continuity." He looked up at me, and locked eyes with me with complete seriousness on his face. "I can't read it." The bond stirred. The words of his confession might have seemed straight-forward, but the bond translated that statement for me. He meant I can't help you. The realization hit him hard.

"Collin…" My fingers brushed the top of his hand to get his attention and break his thoughts before they turned dark. The icy hot spark of skin on skin instantly caught his attention, and had the desired effect. "We'll figure it out."

And I thought we could, but as we sat there for the rest of the night trying to decipher Eric's writing it became more and more obvious that we couldn't.

Collin used his phone to look some things up online, but that didn't help at all. It led us back to our initial impression—this was some derivative of ancient Greek. As he researched, I looked for the page that Eric had showed me before. I saw the scrawling handwriting in black-brown ink that was written with an ancient pen. It was neat, like the old Eric, with everything grouped into rows. Some rows seemed to be grouped in circles, while others seemed like squares.

I had no idea what it meant, but when I found the page I was looking for, I froze. My fingers touched the yellowed parchment gently, as if I couldn't believe the drawing was there—Apryl's necklace. The drawing showed a black and white disc, exactly like mine. There were words around it. What did Eric say this was called? He told me once, and I wanted to know about it. I wanted to know how my sister came into possession of something that belonged to the demon realm while she was alive and well, having nothing to do with demons. The answers were right in front of me, but I couldn't understand what it said.

I pointed to the book and asked Collin, "I saw this page, before when Eric showed me this book. He didn't tell me what was on it at the time, but later, when we were coming to find you—he mentioned my necklace. He said he knew it was brimstone, and that it was called the…" it sounded like Kreturus. I rolled the word in mouth until I recognized it, "The Kreturic Pendant! Do you think we could use that information as a starting place, and see if we can try to see what words say that on this page?"

Collin looked at my necklace and back down at the drawing in the book. "It's worth a try. This is a Kappa," his finger pointed to something that looked like a K and then an N, followed by an E. "This looks like the beginning of Kreturus or Kreturuic, but the word just stops." His fingers trailed quickly over every letter surrounding the drawing, while he spoke softly sounding out each possibility. He did it quickly, and his finger dashed across the page and in several different directions before he sighed and looked up at me. Shaking his head, he said, "It's not here. Whatever language this is, it isn't close enough to Greek to read any of it. It was a good idea Ivy. If it was close enough, it might have worked." He slumped and leaned back against the wall, gripping his forehead in his hands. "Is it spreading?" The question took me by surprise because he never asked me about it.

I looked up at him, while leaving my fingers on the book. "What?"

His face turned up to look at me. There was a weariness there that was growing harder to ignore. "Is the poison from the fang spreading inside of you? Can you tell?"

Without thinking, I pressed my hand to my chest and shook my head. The searing pain of the poison traveling through my body was burned into my memory forever. "No, it's not moving. At least it isn't right now. I'd feel it if it was. The sapphire serum seems to be isolated to this one spot." I pressed my fingers to the top of my left breast, grateful that Lorren crystalized it. But I knew it was slowly leaking into me because effonating had done something to it. I suspected that the heat of effoanting messed with Lorren's crystallization of the serum, but I didn't know for sure. And, I didn't know how much time I had before the poison would kill me. I was hoping that I'd be able to tell before it became critical, since I'd experienced the full brunt of the sapphire serum before.

Collin tilted his head back against the wall. "That's unusual." He let the words hang in the air, and when I didn't reply he added, "Normally the poison would travel through the victim—it spiders out away from the original wound like mold. But yours isn't?" I shook my head. Where was this going? Why was he looking at me like that? Collin stared at me for a few moments. I couldn't sense what he was thinking through the bond, although I reached out for it. He scolded as he felt me intrude into his thoughts, "Ask me, if you want to know. Don't try and press into my mind and steal what I'm thinking."

Feeling sheepish, I looked away and said, "You seem leery of something. I just wanted to know what it was. That's all. I didn't mean to..." I looked up at him. "I'll try not to do it again, but it's difficult to shut out your thoughts and feelings. Sometimes I can't no matter how hard I try."

"Yeah, but right now that isn't what happened. You felt scared and went digging through my mind. Not the same." His words were warning, but I didn't back down so fast.

I pointed at him, "You did the same thing just now!" Smugness rolled off of me. "That's how you knew I felt scared."

He laughed, "No, that wasn't it." Leaning forward, he asked, "Damn, Ivy. Don't you use any of your senses anymore? I looked at you, okay? I see fear in your eyes. Something I said spooked you, so I asked what it was and you responded by diving into my thoughts." Well, that would explain it too. I looked back down at the book, as if it interested me amazingly so.

I shouldn't have pressed into his mind. Privacy was something we both valued, but I wanted it because I was hiding so many secrets. I was beginning to wonder if he was doing the same thing. "You're right," I muttered softly, not wanting to fight with him.

Collin walked over to me, and hovered over the book. Glancing out of the corner of my eye, I saw a smile spread across his face, "What was that, Ivy? Could you speak up? I didn't quite catch those last words."

My smugness evaporated. I shouldn't have pried and he knew it. I had no idea how he was controlling himself and not taking a mind dive when I didn't answer him, but he didn't. I hated admitting I was wrong, and he knew it. "Fine," I said, not taking my eyes off the book, "you deserve to gloat. You were right. I was wrong."

His fingers wrapped around my waist as he came up behind me. "What's that? I can't hear you!" The instant he said those words, he started tickling me. I jerked away from the book, swatting at his hands.

I tried to pull away from him to turn around, but he wouldn't let me. His fingers gently touched my waist and spots around my ribcage that were so ticklish that I couldn't stand up. Laughing so hard I thought I'd pee, I leaned into him and tickled him back.

"I'm always right!" I laughed, "And you're always wrong!" With that his fingers dug in mercilessly and I laughed so hard tears formed in my eyes.

Collin pushed me back onto the floor, as I swatted his advances and attempted a counterattack, but he wasn't as ticklish as I was. I kicked and wiggled, repeating myself and teasing him—basically taunting him to continue tickling me until I passed out. I made one last attempt to bring ticklish tears to his eyes, but before I knew it, he grabbed my wrists and pinned me to the floor. Breathless and laughing, he hovered over me. Joy was radiating off of him so intense that I couldn't ignore it. His eyes had crinkles in the corners, as his rich laughter filled the boathouse. His hair hung in his eyes as he looked down at me, and I smiled back up at him, still giggling. I was on the verge of having uncontrollable giggles and noticed that I hadn't felt like this in years. Laughter wasn't something I'd had in large quantities lately. There'd been so many months of despair and sorrow. All of that misery was burnt up in the hysterical giggles in a matter of seconds.

Smile on my face, I teased, "You like it when I'm right."

Blue eyes blazing, he replied, "I LOVE it when you're right. The smirk you get on your face is priceless. And then you try not to say anything," he laughed, "as if you could possibly be humble! Take credit where credit's due, Ivy. Everyone can see it on your face anyway." He smiled down at me, inches from my face. "Take what's yours."

"Hmmmm," was the only thing I said, as I agreed with him. My tickling fingers stopped jabbing and poking, and threaded through his soft brown hair as I pulled him closer to me. The smile on his face faltered and softened, as he neared my lips. I released his hair and ran my fingers down the side of his face, enjoying the sensation of his warm breath on my skin.

Smiling softly I said, "You're mine," and leaned up and pressed my lips against his.

It was strange how everything went from being light and playful to hot and heavy in a matter of seconds. His words had almost sounded like a dare to me, as if he were telling me to kiss him. Up until now, he kissed me. I'd never initiated a kiss, other than the first time when he turned me down. His silky lips pressed against my mouth, as he lowered himself on top of me. The button on my jeans dug into my skin at an odd angle, but I didn't want to stop or ask him to move. Apparently, he was thought-peeking, because he shifted his weight and the brass button no longer hurt. His hands ran up and down my sides, sliding onto the small of my back as he pulled me closer to him and the kiss deepened. My pulse shot up higher and higher the longer he touched me.

Collin was breathless in my arms, as I slid my hands under his shirt. The warmth of his skin slid beneath my fingers. Collin's body arched slightly at the touch, as if I'd surprised him, and he suddenly pulled away from me. It felt like I couldn't breathe when his lips left mine. I'd hoped his mouth would have lingered and moved to my neck, and his hands would… I was so euphoric that I didn't see the worry on his face.

After he pulled back, he gently whispered, "I don't want to hurt you."

Breathless, I asked, "What? You won't," but he continued to pull away from me and sat up. "Collin…?"

His hands shook, as he pushed the hair out of his face. Something frazzled him. Not looking at me for a moment, he cleared his throat, and stood up. When his gaze returned to me, I had sat up and was feeling badly about him not wanting me. "It's not like that, and you know it." He said gently. "Damn, Ivy," he smiled wickedly at me, while extending his hand, "you make me totally crazy. I've never wanted anything in my entire life as much as I want you right now."

Taking his offered hand, I let him pull me up. I still felt uncertain, because he pulled away from me so fast, but I tried to bury the feelings. Collin said he was reading my face, but I knew he could read my thoughts. He could read my emotions too if he touched me, and his hands were just all over me. He had to know that his actions made me feel rejected. I didn't really understand why he kept pulling away. Part of me wanted to be with him. The other part of me thought that was terrifying and slightly insane.

CHAPTER TWENTY-FIVE

Maybe Collin recovered quickly from our lustfest, or maybe he didn't. I couldn't tell and I promised I wouldn't go digging around in his thoughts anymore, so I tried to stay out. It was difficult, because I wanted to know what he was thinking. I wanted to know the real reason he pulled away. It couldn't have been because he thought he'd hurt me. Collin was the only Valefar who was able to control his bloodlust. The rest would have sucked my soul dry long ago, but he didn't. Maybe I was a tease. Maybe I was pushing him too hard. I glanced over at him, and he smiled back at me, taking my hand in his.

We were sitting at St. Bart's in the kitchen. Al was the only one there with us. It was risky to keep returning to the church, but I didn't know who else to ask. If anyone would know what language Eric's notes were written in, it would be her.

When asked about the other Martis, she answered, "Julia's called every Martis to action. They're doing something, and I told 'em they could do it without the likes of me." She stirred her tea cup, looking at the center, but I was sure she didn't see anything. Her mind was lost in thought, but she startled herself back to reality and saw Collin and I staring at her. "There aren't many new Martis forming, which limit our numbers greatly. The number of Valefar in this area alone has skyrocketed. It's odd that there aren't a proportionate number of new Martis to handle the problem. Julia is checking with every Martis compound worldwide, looking for new Martis, but there have been no reports of new blood. There hasn't been a new Martis reported since, well, since you were marked, Ivy." She gestured at me.

Collin's gaze cut from me to Al, confused at the information. "Ivy was marked over six months ago, though. Aren't there usually dozens of new Martis chosen during that much time?"

Al nodded, "Yes, there are. A dozen minimum, but with what's happening, it should have been many, many more. But, Julia can't find record of even one. It spooked her, so she pulled all the Martis home to Rome, with only sentries remaining at their old posts."

My eyes went wide, "There aren't any Martis here? They're all gone? Every single one?" She nodded, "And you're the sentry, aren't you?" A half smile smirked across her face. I laughed, "You crafty old nun, you! You stayed so you could help me?" I leaned forward, half exclaiming, half asking.

Her silvery eyes met mine. She tilted her head at me as she laid her spoon next to the untouched cup of tea. "Of course I did! I couldn't leave you to rot. I had no idea when you'd be back, but I knew you needed someone to help anchor you to yourself. You have a tendency to drift, you know?"

I snorted, "That's an understatement. But, I'm glad you stayed. I know I need you, and all the things you know. You say things to me that very few people would have the guts to say." I shrugged not wanting to get all mushy. "So, what's Julia doing, then? Why would she move all the Martis? What does she think is happening?" This had so many possibilities and sparked so many questions that I didn't know where to begin.

Al looked between me and Collin, "I don't know, but the angels only stopped creating more Martis at one other point in history—when they trapped Kreturus in the Underworld and overtook a portion of Hell. After that, they thought the battle was over and let our numbers dwindle. Angels don't like messing with the natural order of things and plucking some squirrelly kid from their life to fight in an immortal's war is kinda disruptive." She winked at me, and I nodded back. I was resentful that they'd chosen me. At the same time, if an angel hadn't given me my mark it was possible that I'd be dead now, or a Valefar. Jake's attack wasn't very forgiving. "When the angels realized that the Valefar were running amuck here, they saw the need to continue creating Martis over the centuries, so they did. The angels always made more Martis—until now."

My eyes were wide. This was weird. Why would I be the last person the angels turned Martis? What were they doing?

Collin articulated my questions before I could ask. "So, there's no way to know what the angels are doing? There's no way to ask? Because, this looks bad Althea. It looks like your kind is being..." he swallowed, not wanting to finish the sentence. A mixture of emotions was flowing from Collin, thick and uncensored. I sensed them immediately without meaning to, and looked over at him. He returned my gaze with worry in his eyes.

Al finished his thought for him, "Like we're being deserted." Her sterling eyes looked sharply at me. "Yes, it would seem that way. And no, there aren't any angels here to ask. Unlike the demons that control your kind, the angels left us to do what's best and fulfill our common goals without them."

The corner of Collin's lip pulled up in disbelief as his eyebrows pulled together, "They didn't leave any of their kind here? How are you supposed to contact them if you need help?" His voice rose as he spoke. It was like he couldn't believe the good guys had such incompetent commanders.

Al's gaze darted back to Collin, "We don't. The system operates on trust. We trust them, they trust us." She took a sip of tea and clinked the old cup against the saucer when she put it back down. Her hands were shaking. I'd never seen her like this before. She was always so self-assure, always certain that things would end well. A knot formed in my stomach and twisted tighter and tighter as the conversation continued.

"Al, that makes no sense. What does trust have to do with anything? The angels have more power. They could come here and end all this stuff, but they don't. Besides, the Martis have been screwing things up for years, and the angels didn't return. Will they really just leave things the way they are?" Collin turned to me, mouth hanging open at my outburst.

Al just looked at me with sympathetic eyes and smiled, "It worked well for several millennia. The entire system is based on trust; trust the angels to choose the right people, trust that we will transform them into equipped Martis to deal with the Valefar, and trust that we'll handle things here while they handle things there." She saw the look on my face and added, "I know you don't understand, dear girl. You've had so much taken from you unfairly, no doubt, that it's hindered you badly."

Bristling at her words my spine went straight. "I'm not broken. I'm not the monster they think I am. It's not going to happen." I said the words staccato, enunciating each one clearly.

Collin's hand slid over mine as he gently brushed a thought against my mind, *That's not what she said. She believes in you.* He smiled at me. Al watched the two of us closely before he added, "And so do I." Smiling at him softly, I nodded, apologized to Al, and slumped back in my seat folding my arms across my chest.

Al sipped her tea before saying, "Things are beyond comprehension now, Ivy. All we have is faith—faith that the person sitting next us will do the right thing—no matter what it is. No matter what it costs. We both know you're that girl; the one who does what's right no matter what. Don't forget who you are, and you have nothing to worry about. Anchor yourself to people who'll remind you of that, and ignore the words of others. They don't matter," Al said with utter certainty. I nodded. It was an easy thing to say, but much harder to actually do.

Collin cleared his throat, and tapped at the book on the table. "Althea, we found Eric's book, but the language predates my existence. We were hoping you could read it." He slid the book across the table to the nun. She'd looked at it when we first arrived but didn't pepper us with questions about it. She had patience that I lacked, because curiosity would have prompted me to ask what it was as soon as I saw it.

Al's withered old hands reached out for the old book. She turned it towards her and ran her fingers over the worn leather cover. When she opened it, it made the sound that old books with thick pages make—where it almost sounds as if the spine were cracking. Gently, she opened to a yellowed page and examined the contents.

In that moment, it felt like I stopped breathing. This was it. This is what would allow me to find out about the Satan Stone, so I could heal the sapphire serum in my chest. Collin's fingers gently intertwined with mine and he squeezed my hand under the table. He looked over at me, smiling softly. I returned the squeeze and smiled back before leaning forward. Collin was emitting a sense of foreboding, as if he knew what would happen long before I did. The old woman leaned over the book for what seemed like a lifetime, and then turned an ancient page, saying nothing.

Impatience got the better of me, "Well, what does it say?" Al knew everything. She was older than Eric, hell, she was there when Eric found out he was a Martis. She knew him nearly his entire life. She had to recognize his handwriting. He was her favorite. I remembered her smiling up at him with overwhelming pride. She trained him. She taught him everything he knew—how to be a Martis, how to fight, how to track, hunt, and win. If anyone could read Eric's scrawling handwriting, it would be her. I was so hopeful that she would know and be able to tell us what it said right then. I lowered my head to catch her gaze.

She saw me and looked up from the book and shook her head. "No idea. I can't read this at all. It's like it's Koine Greek," she looked up at me, "Greek spoken around the time Eric was born. Greek spoken by common folk back then. It's kinda like street talk in that it has no formality to it. But," she shook her head, "that's not what this is." She sounded surprised that she couldn't read it, but Collin wasn't.

He nodded, "I thought it was Greek as well, an earlier version, but still Greek. But it's not. The characters may be of Greek origin, or maybe they just look the same..." he reached over and slid the book towards him, turning to the page with the drawing of my necklace. "This is Ivy's pendant—the one hanging on her necklace. Eric mentioned that he knew the pendant had brimstone on it and that it was the Kreturic Pendant. We think these are his notes on the subject, but there is no commonality with either word. There were no matches for Kreturus or brimstone. He would have made a notation like that on the page, but there's nothing here." He pushed the book back to Al so she could see.

Her gnarled fingers trailed over the page as she nodded. "You're right," Al replied, shaking her head. "We could have used that as a benchmark to translate this thing, but there isn't anything that even resembles those words. Half the characters in here seem to be made up. They aren't Greek at all…and it's not an issue of bad penmanship." She bit her lips as she thought, staring at the paper.

My heart went from elation to plummeting into my toes. Things were about to get bad. I needed that translation. I needed to know about Satan's Stone and how to find it. Stealing a glance at Collin, I felt a lump grow in my throat. It can't come to a demon kiss. I won't let it. Desperation filled me. "We have to figure out what this says." My voice was faint, and low. Irritation shot through me. If Eric were here, if he were himself, this wouldn't be an issue. But, he wasn't. He was a lusty Valefar now. I pressed my eyes closed and shook my head. Collin put his hand on my shoulder to calm me. I smiled at him, but didn't want him experiencing my emotional hurricane with me, so I backed away from him and paced across the room. After a few walks around the tiny yellow kitchen with the faded floral wallpaper, I stopped and leaned against the sink.

"Ah, Ivy," Al said, not looking up from the book. "Things aren't always what they seem."

I suppressed the urge to roll my eyes. I wasn't in the mood for fortune cookie talk. "What do you mean," I asked point blank.

She looked up at me, smiling. "This is a code, that's all. He coded his notes so no one else could read them. Clever boy..." Al was delighted. "It prevents Valefar, or anyone else, from using the information for the wrong reason. He tracked you for nearly two millennia, Ivy. At one time, books were things only the wealthy owned. A poor boy like Eric with a thick book like this looked suspicious...But a book written in gibberish—who would want it?"

Collin stood and walked around the table to look over Al's shoulder, comprehension lighting up his face. "That sneaky bastard," he said softly with a smile spreading across his face.

I sighed and they looked up at me. "It still doesn't help if Eric was the only person who could read it."

That was the plain cold hard truth. I couldn't get the information on Satan's Stone, sapphire serum, or anything unless we could read that book. And knowing Eric, the old Eric, he would have made the code unbreakable and not just gibberish at first sight.

Collin looked up at me, "We should at least try. It's not like we can trap Eric and have him read it for us anyway. He can't remember any of this." Collin tapped the page in front of him.

A thought occurred to me and I straightened, "But he remembers some things." They both looked up at me, with a slight glace at one another. "Well, he remembers how to speak English and it's not his first language—that old Greek was. So what's to say he doesn't remember it? Or how he coded this book? Maybe he still knows that information." The thought bounced around in my head more. Apryl had remembered things she should have forgotten. The thoughts pushed to the surface and she remembered me. She'd said it was because she thought of me when she was looking at Eric, but that was all we needed. Just a glimmer of a memory, and Eric could read what he wrote in this book. A smile started to spread across my face, but was quickly dashed by Al's words.

"We can't give this book to Eric, now." She looked alarmed that I even suggested it. "If he did have information in here about Satan's Stone, he could use it for himself. We can't risk giving it to him, even if he might remember how to read it."

Walking towards them, I put my hands on the table and leaned in, "But, we could just show him a page—the page with the pendant—and ask him to read it. If he could, that would give us enough information to decode the rest of it, right?" They both looked at each other and then back at me, too hesitant to nod.

Hesitation was clear on his face. Collin walked towards me and took my hands in his, "If we had to, we could trap Eric and force him to tell us how he coded it. But, I can't see him giving us that information even if he does know it. And I'm not sure it's worth the risk to try. Ivy, Al's right. We don't know what these pages say. If they contain things that could give him more power—anything at all, then we should never let him near this book. Any of it." I listened to what Collin was saying, and maybe he was right, but I didn't think so. It was worth the risk, because I knew something that they didn't. Eric faltered. He was afraid of me.

Certainty shot through me. I decided and there was no stopping me. I'd fix this mess and move on with tracking down Kreturus, the demonic bastard, and ending this. Last time I saw him, I faltered. He took Collin from me in a way I couldn't even imagine. It shocked me to my core. But next time, I would face Kreturus alone. Placing my hand on Collin's shoulder, I said, "We did things your way before. We're doing this my way this time. If you guys can't decode it by tomorrow night, I'm going to trap Eric and make him decode it for us."

CHAPTER TWENTY-SIX

Al completely disagreed with my plan. She let me know it too. "You don't know what's on this page," she said smacking a finger against the old parchment. We were still in the old kitchen. We had been at it for hours. Between spouts of nonstop silent frustration at trying to read the unreadable book, there were stints of rather loud frustration directed at me. Mostly by Al. "What if the page has the information you want on it?" Her silvery eyes were brilliant as she argued. "You'd be giving it straight to him! And the last two times you saw Eric, he bested you! Twice! Ivy, you can't possibly think this is a good idea, on any level." We'd been having this conversation for a while, and it was going in circles.

Collin was ignoring us, knowing I would do what I thought was best and that the best thing for him to do was to try and decode Eric's writing before tonight.

"Al, this is the best page to use. We already know what's on it, what the thing in the drawing is called, and the person who told me that was Eric. It will give us something to gauge his translation against. If we use another page, we don't know what's on that either, and we have no idea about anything on it at all—this page, we at least know it's about my necklace." She wrinkled her nose at me, ready to shoot off more words when I cut her off, "Al, it's not totally stupid. Collin and I can trap him. He'll read the page and we'll…"

She raised an eyebrow at me, "You'll what? Let him go? Ivy, Eric's a Valefar now. He'll kill you if he has the chance. You can't trust anything he says. That's why this whole shindig is ridiculous!" She slammed her hands on the old table, causing it to shake as she stood. "This is an unnecessary risk that don't need to be taken, not when you know what you know." Her gaze cut to Collin, and then back to me.

I opened my mouth to argue with her more, but she swished an arm at me and hobbled away irate. She knew about what Lorren said. I'd thought about the angel since then. I wondered why Al didn't tell Collin that there was an angel we could talk to, but I wasn't going to bring him up. That would be completely stupid. Looking over at Collin, worried he'd sense my thoughts, I saw he was still busily trying to decode the page. He had several pages of notes, but nothing that was usable. He glanced up at me and smiled before returning to his work. How could I tell him that I needed my soul back? And oh yeah, by the way—I'm taking yours too. Collin fought to get that tiny scrap of himself back. It was astounding that he spilt his tiny piece of rancid soul to save me, but he did. Collin was…I pressed my eyes closed, unable to even consider telling him that remedy. No. There had to be another way. And there was. And this was it. My plan to trap Eric had to work. Period.

CHAPTER TWENTY-SEVEN

Collin and Al worked on the page, but got nowhere. While they were busy with that, I sat in the study thinking of how to lure Eric out and trap him. He was playing dirty, from what Collin told me. Using his blood when he kidnapped me last time was dangerous for him and me. Collin acted like he didn't understand why Eric did it at all. At least that's what it seemed like at the time. When I asked him about it, I had to twist his arm pretty hard to get him to talk. For some reason speaking of Valefar blood and dark magic worried him. I could feel fear growing inside of him, and it brushed the bond as he was unable to control it at times.

It may have been insane to go looking for Eric. I could admit to that. After all, he had the opportunity to kill me twice now. And both times, he chose not to. I didn't think it was because he forgave me. I wasn't stupid, but there was some hesitation within him. I could sense it. I was counting on that tiny spark of uncertainty to make my plan work. Eric would speak to me. He had to. My plan had to work. There were no more choices, and as long as I was in this weakened state, Kreturus could attack and I'd go down without a fight. This was the only way.

Night fell and when the time came to set the trap for Eric, I revealed my plans to Collin and Al. Al sat there, not saying much, but didn't argue with me any longer. She thought I was taking an unnecessary risk, but I wasn't. I couldn't sacrifice Collin like that. And I knew that I had to be careful with Eric. I didn't bind him when I had the chance. It was mostly because I thought he was dead, but given the chance to bind him now, I would still decline. Something inside of me told me that binding Eric was a mistake, even if it put me in danger. Tonight, Eric would come looking for me, and he'd find me. Collin and Al had Celestial Silver chains that we'd use to trap him and keep him from effonating away.

My plan was fairly simple. Eric wanted me for his own sadistic reasons. We needed someplace where I'd be out in the open alone, but still somewhere that it seemed like the encounter was an accident. We'd make Eric think he caught me. Then, when he tried to take me, Collin and Al would chain him. The old nun assured me she could move fast enough to keep him from leaving with me. And Collin seconded that opinion. This was the part of my plan that was hard for me. I had to believe that they'd get to me fast enough and that if something did go wrong, that they could fix it before Eric snatched me. I thought the plan was simple enough. Al muttered it was too simple, but that was the point. If it looked like we were just out and about, Eric wouldn't suspect an ambush. And even if Eric used his blood and tried to do the same thing as before, we'd have him. There was no way he could escape with me this time.

We put the plan into effect. I left the church building, unshrouded by shadows so that there was nothing masking my scent. Eric would find me faster that way, but so would other Valefar. It was increasingly rare for me to walk around without being shrouded. The shadows were like a cloak shielding me from those who'd drink my soul. But the shadows' presence left a chill deep within me that wasn't warmed in their absence. It had grown permanent, so that I was always cold. I wondered if that was the poison amplifying the shadows' effects, but there was no way to know.

Leaving the safety of the church, Collin helped me into his car and we drove to the diner—the one I had met Eric at so long ago. The diner shimmered. It was a silvery beacon in the middle of the dark night. As Collin slid into the booth, I slid in opposite him. He was agitated that he agreed to go through with this. I could feel it wafting off of him. Instead of being offended, I placed my hand over his until he looked up into my eyes.

I smiled softly at him, and whispered, "I love you."

His anger faded as he took my hand in his. "I love you, too. But I don't know if I can do this, Ivy. I can't stand the thought of something happening to you." Collin rubbed his fingers gently against the back of my hand while he spoke softly. "What if he's more powerful than we thought? He already showed that he's mastered some of the vilest magic that we're capable of. What if he's not the same for some reason? Ivy…" his voice trailed off and he shook his head.

I interrupted, "But he is the same. He's a Valefar. You know everything about Valefar. You know their strengths and their limits. You commanded the ones in this area for a long time. I'd think that this would be predictable for you. But I can see on your face, you think it's not."

He shook his head, "Never think anyone is predictable—especially him." We were intentionally not using Eric's name so we wouldn't tip him off. If someone overheard our conversation, it could easily sound like we were talking about Kreturus or another Valefar. Collin's back straightened as he accepted I was going through with this no matter what. Both of his hands gripped mine, "Remember, if something goes wrong…you know what to do. I'll heal you." The plan was if anything—anything at all—went wrong, I was supposed to effonate back to St. Bart's. Collin would follow me there, and already had the coal and milk mixture ready.

He tilted his head, looking into my eyes. "Okay?"

I smiled at him. I'd made up most of this plan. He and Al tweaked it where it had weaknesses so that Eric couldn't carry me off. I nodded, "I can do it. No problem. And later tonight, we'll have enough of that translated that we can figure out how to fix this whole mess." My hand rested on my chest near the site of the sapphire serum. Collin's eyes lingered there for a moment before coming back up to my face.

The conversation shifted, and we continued to talk and laugh like nothing in the world could possibly be wrong. I only hoped that Eric was still following me. I knew he'd take the chance to catch me alone, and that he'd do it at the most opportune time for him. After we ordered, I took my cue and smiled at Collin. My heart was racing in my chest. I kissed his cheek and said, "Be back in a second," knowing that this was it. Eric would show up as soon as I was out of sight. As I walked away, I mouthed over my shoulder, I love you. Collin needed reassurance, but Al couldn't sit out here with him. She was already in place, waiting.

My boots clicked on the checkerboard tiles, as I walked to the back of the diner to the ladies room. I passed an old guy holding a cup of steaming coffee in his enormous hands. He nodded as I passed, and returned his gaze to his newspaper. He had no idea what was about to happen. He'd sit out here and drink his coffee while a depraved Valefar was a stone's throw away. My heart began to crawl up into my throat with each step. Every time I passed another booth, my throat grew tighter and tighter. The last people that I walked past were a young couple with shiny new wedding bands. They were sitting on the same side of the booth with their heads tilted together, whispering, and laughing softly. They were lost in bliss, unaware of the terrible things that were about to go down around them.

Before I pushed the door open to walk in, I looked back at Collin. His thought brushed my mind, *You don't have to do this. We'll find another way.*

I answered back, *There is no other way. I can do this. I promise. Just come when I call you.*

With that, I pushed the door open and disappeared inside. Bare bulbs hung over a huge mirror and illuminated the room. The bathroom was fairly clean for such a busy restaurant. I looked around. The room had a large grated window that was closed and two red stalls. No one was here. Good. Pressing my eyes closed, I stood in front of the mirror. I placed my hands gently on the cold counter, and breathed deeply.

The metallic scrape was so faint that I almost didn't hear it. The back of my neck prickled and I could sense he was behind me, but I didn't look up. When Eric leaned forward, closer to me, his breath touched the back of my neck, and I startled and spun around. A wicked smile spread across his lips.

"Remember me?" he asked pressing me against the counter the second I turned toward him, using his body to trap me. I leaned back, arching my back over the countertop, unable to get away from him.

Momentarily stunned, I froze. For some reason, seeing him like this was worse than anything else that'd happened to me. Loosing those two seconds, the two seconds that I stood there motionless caused my plan to crumble. I was supposed to call to Collin using the bond. He was near enough to hear me. Al was somewhere nearby, waiting to pounce. As soon as I head the metallic click of the bathroom door locking, I should have called Collin. But I didn't. Something inside me froze, as if it broke and no longer had any desire to continue on with our plan.

Eric's legs pressed me into the counter as he leaned closer. The back of the Formica countertop bit into my thighs through my jeans, but I couldn't move. Closing his eyes, he inhaled deeply. Eric's eyes had been gold seconds ago, but now I doubted that they stayed that way. His body was so tense that all his muscles were flexed as he tried his best to control himself. Desire wafted off of him, raw and bold. I expected him to be incoherent with blood red eyes, but when he pulled away, I was surprised to see his irises shift back to gold with a flicker. What was that? Did he learn to control his lust?

All these things seemed like they were taking place in a vat of Jell-O. My words, my breath, everything seemed to take longer and last longer than I thought possible, as if they were inexplicably suspended in air and moving slower than physics allowed. Later, I'd find out that everything happened in a matter of terrifying seconds.

"Eric," I breathed with my heart racing in my chest. He looked down at me, and my breath caught in my throat. His eyes were so golden that I couldn't look away. They were beautiful. Suddenly, I had the sinking feeling that I was no longer in control of the situation. I tried to call out to Collin with my mind, but couldn't. I couldn't do anything, but stare at Eric with open-mouthed desire. What was happening? Why couldn't I think? Why couldn't I move? I tried to break my gaze from his beautiful eyes, but I couldn't. That was when I heard something slam into the door. A burst of heat erupted to my right, and Al materialized from someplace unseen, but I didn't care. I stood there, transfixed, staring at Eric.

The locked door cost Collin half a second, if that, but Al was already in the room wildly casting silver chains at Eric. The chains danced as if they were alive and wrapped themselves around Eric's shoulders, pulling his arms snuggly away from me. When Collin entered the room, the first thing he did was pull me away from Eric, but my feet wouldn't move. The room swam and I fell to the floor. Collin looked down at me, concerned, but he had to help Al. It appeared that Eric was shirking off the chains.

"Pull them! Now!" Collin yelled. The noise of chain rattling and the screams of Eric drew attention to the restroom. Soon there were voices demanding we unlock the door, followed by the pounding of fists when we didn't comply.

Al pulled her chains tight at the same time as Collin. It was like watching someone trap a dangerous animal. Eric snarled, and his eyes burned bright red as he tried to lash out at them, but he was unable to because his arms were bound tightly to his side. It seemed like it was over, but I knew it wasn't. Power was wafting off of Eric—it had to be. I was still enthralled with him, watching his every movement—neither hoping we'd catch him or that he'd free himself—it didn't matter to me. I just felt the need to watch him; to watch his smooth muscles flex as he twisted and turned under the chains. No one noticed me sitting there. Collin thought I was hurt. Concern spilled through the bond from him, but he didn't realize what was wrong with me or how severe it really was.

Pulling the chains tight—a movement that normally burnt a Valefar's flesh and beat them into submission—was the action that killed the rest of my plan. At the yank of the silver chains, they constricted tightly around Eric's entire body, hissing while they burned welts into his flesh. But the chains didn't hold. The added stress from yanking the chain caused the tiny links that made the silver chain to shatter. There was a spray of tiny silver pieces as they tinkled and clinked, and they fell to the floor.

Al and Collin stared at each other in horror.

Eric lunged for me, and I did nothing to stop him. He laughed and slid his bleeding thumb along my lower lip. Without a thought, eagerness overcame me and I ran my tongue over his precious blood, wishing I could have more.

Collin screamed as he flung himself at us, but Eric laughed, "She's mine now."

Collin's hand wrapped around my wrist, but he was too late. I was already dissolving as heat flashed through me. Collin's wide blue eyes watched me in terror as I was carried away in Eric's arms.

CHAPTER TWENTY-EIGHT

Effonation sucked when I didn't have a lethal poison lodged in my chest, but doing it with the sapphire serum made it unbearable. My body resisted the pain as long as possible, but it was impossible to ignore. Fighting the pain quickly drained every drop of energy I had, and sleep began to paw at me, making my eyelids droop. My head feel too heavy to hold up. I passed out as soon as the pain from the heat stopped. Drowsiness overtook me and I felt my body go limp in Eric's arms. I was too out of it to be terrified. Nothing mattered at that second. I was too weak and the pain from having my skin spliced off left me numb this time.

Semiconscious, I felt Eric carrying me as he clicked through a door and laid me down where I slept like the dead, unaware of what has happening.

Sleep was scaring me more and more. Every time that healing sleep was needed, my dreams grew stranger and stranger. This time was no different. When the darkness cleared, I found myself in a grand room. The intricate marble floors gleamed under candle light. High on a shelf, I spied the only object in the entire room - a gleaming ruby challis. Suddenly, my mouth was filled with sand and the tiny grains flowed from my lips and onto the floor in front of me. As soon as I decided that I needed that cup to fill with water, the sand stopped. I moved toward the shelf and felt a long black ball gown swishing around my ankles. I looked down, realizing I was wearing a tightly laced black corset with large stone decorations that flowed into the black skirt.

Ignoring the gown, I reached for the crimson cup on the shelf. My fingers wrapped around the cold crystal, and I peered inside. It was filled with silver liquid. Putting the challis to my lips, I drank greedily until the shining liquid was gone. At first, the liquid quenched my thirst, so when the cup refilled, I drank more. But after two cups of the shimmering silver drink, it turned rancid in my mouth as it solidified. As I gagged on the course drink, it felt like I was going to vomit. Opening my mouth wide and dry heaving, the contents of my stomach finally erupted in the form of black feathers. Grackles erupted from the feathers and flew from my mouth making hideous screeches, as they flew away. When there was nothing left to heave up from my stomach, I looked at the cup in my hand. It had turned into a snake and coiled around my shoulders as if it knew me.

I screamed, trying to take it off, but a voice said, *You cannot deny what you are.*

Confused I stopped struggling and looked up. The snake had melded with my skin, and it bared its poisoned fangs. The rest of the snake's body dissolved into mine. Slack jawed, I watched in horror as my skin was replaced with cold scales, and my eye teeth grew into long, curved fangs filled with venom.

Sweat covered my entire body as I sat up screaming. White sheets were stuck to me, and sweat dribbled down my temples. Wildly, I threw back the blankets, remembering what happened, and tried to stand. My body protested and I fell to the floor, landing square on my hip. Tears streamed down my face, as a hand grasped my arm and picked me up. Before I knew what happened, arms were around me and lifting me back into the bed. There was such a thick haze over my eyes that I could barely see anything. Blinking back tears, I looked at the person standing next to me.

Eric.

His body was long and lean. Since he turned Valefar, he was dressing differently. It defined his sleek body and the curves of his muscles. His golden eyes peered down at me, cold and lifeless. "You are one pain in the ass, Taylor." I winced as he spoke. His voice seemed so loud. His eyes narrowed as he stared at me, folding his arms over his chest.

I held my hands to my forehead. The throbbing sensation in my temples was horrible, and the light seemed blinding, although I knew it was fairly dark in here. Something was wrong. Trying to look up at him defiantly, I growled, "What'd you do to me?"

The corner of Eric's mouth pulled up into a crooked smile. It reminded me of the old Eric, but with an evil twist. "Blood. What else?" He shook his head, shocked that I didn't know. "Do you seriously not know?" I shook my head and instantly regretted it.

"I feel like I have a hangover," my fingertips pressed into my temples as I looked down. Nausea washed over me as I pressed my lips closed. I'd not done any serious partying in a long time, but I recognized the effects. Damn, did he drug me? Anger erupted inside of me. I shot off the bed and threw a punch at his stomach, "You drugged me, you sick bastard."

Eric laughed, easily grabbing my wrist and twisting it until I screamed and fell back onto the bed. I lay on my back, staring at the ceiling, too weak and nauseous to move. Eric leaned next to me. "Tell me why your boyfriend has no idea what Valefar blood can do. How could that be possible?" I didn't know what he was talking about and told him so. "That's just it. He should have known not to risk you, but he did anyway. What do you want so badly that it would be worth risking you?"

I turned slowly towards Eric. The room swirled around him before settling. I pressed my eyes closed, willing it to stop spinning. That was when I felt warm fingers press gently on my eyes, and before Eric said, "Open." I did as he said, and the spinning stopped. Blinking, I looked at him.

His short hair had grown out since the last time I saw him. He didn't wear it neat and parted anymore. It was wild and messy. The dark clothing he wore made his skin seem paler, but it made his eyes glow bright gold. Eric's mouth twitched into another smile, "Like what you see?"

My stomach fluttered and I looked away. I moved to sit up and Eric didn't try to stop me. The room no longer spun at all, but my head was still throbbing. "If you didn't drug me, then what'd you do to me?"

Eric sighed and sat up next to me. "Blood, Taylor. You're an addict now. Get used to it." He rose and walked over to a bookcase. The room I was in was very different from the last skeevy hotel room he took me to. This room was almost completely white, with dark wood floors, and white fluffy throw rugs scattered about. I was laid on a huge dark wood poster bed with white linens in the center of the room.

My jaw tensed, "What? What are you talking about? I'm not hooked on anything." In the past, that might have been a different story —some could have said I was hooked on boys and used them like a drug— but not now. My heart was racing, and I felt strange, like I needed something, but I wasn't sure what. The strange dreams... Being covered in sweat... My mouth hung open, ready to ask what he did to me, but too afraid to. I was acting like I was addicted to something.

Eric didn't shy away from the subject, though he wasn't gloating either. "You're addicted to my blood. You want it. That's why you feel like that. That's why you couldn't move when I captured you." He walked back to the bed where I was sitting and stood in front of me. "How did he not tell you how this works? What reason could he possibly have for not telling you?" An evil smile spread across his lips as he tilted his head at me, "Are you hooked on his blood, too?"

"No!" Rage flew through me. Collin didn't drug me so I would like him. I never felt like this with him— I never felt out of control and twitchy. But, why didn't he tell me? A frown slid across my face. What was

Collin hiding? Something that had to do with blood… I tried to piece it together, but I didn't know.

Glancing up at Eric, I asked, "What does it do?" When Eric only looked at me and said nothing, I felt desperate. He trapped me and had some power over me now. Shit! Why didn't Collin tell me this! Anger coursed through me and I balled my fists, ready to rip Eric apart. But I was too weak, and he knew it.

He finally dropped his folded arms, and spoke, "It's like a drug. You'll crave my blood and want more. And you already know the rest—the more Valefar blood you ingest, the more likely you'll become one of us."

All the breath was sucked from my body. The pit of my stomach went cold as I bent in half, grabbing my stomach. A storm of emotions erupted inside of me. Why didn't Collin tell me? Why did Eric do this? I should have listened to Al. I screamed, and looked up at him. My eyes pooled violet. I could feel the heat in every inch of my body.

"Take it away. Undo it. Now," I hissed.

Eric stood in front of me and was completely unprepared for what happened next. I launched myself at him, but this time my attempt wasn't halfhearted. My fingers grabbed my silver comb, elongating the blades as I threw myself at him. The silver tines ripped across his chest as he attempted to move, but he wasn't fast enough. The momentum of my movement sent us flying across the room when our bodies collided. I had extra power, but I was unsure of where it came from or how long it would last. I didn't care. For the instant, I was much stronger than Eric. I pinned him to the floor with ease. Inhaling sharply, I swung back my comb, ready to thrust the blades through his throat. Ribbons of blood flowed from the hissing wound in his chest, and filled the air with an alluring aroma.

Transfixed, I stared at the wound, with my weapon poised over my right shoulder, ready to sever his neck. In that moment, I saw what I was—who I'd become. Anger filled my body, and mingled with lust for the boy's blood—the boy who was pinned beneath me— the boy who saved my life more than once—the boy I turned Valefar.

Disgust crept through me as my thoughts collided with my actions. The weight of my arms grew so heavy and I was so disgusted with myself. The silver slipped from my fingers and the comb clattered to the floor. Sliding off of Eric, I sat down hard and pushed my flaming purple hair out of my face. What was I doing? I didn't want to kill Eric. What was I doing? Fear coursed through my body wildly, subduing the anger. Swallowing hard, I looked up at him. Eric sat across from me, watching. He said nothing. He didn't move, or do any of the things that I'd expect the new Eric to do. He just sat opposite me, with his jaw hanging open slightly, watching me.

My fingers threaded through my hair and pulled. After a few seconds I couldn't tolerate his gaze anymore. "You know exactly what you're doing! You always have, Eric. You're so damn smart that I was glad we were on the same side before—even though you hated my guts for most of that time." I pulled my hair out of my face and drew my knees up to my chest, wrapping my arms around my ankles.

"Mmmm. But, I was wrong. It didn't matter how smart I was because I was just severely wrong." He hesitated before asking, "My blood had no effect on you just then? Did it?"

Staring at him, stunned, I replied without thinking, "I wanted it, but it didn't stop me." I could admit that I was an addict. It wasn't my fault that Eric forced blood down my throat. I wanted his blood, but something else was dominating me.

"What did?" Eric asked.

Swallowing hard, I knew exactly what stopped me, but I wasn't telling him that. Becoming the sword yielding bitch that kills everyone scared me more than anything. And again, Eric was proof that I was capable of becoming her completely. Not killing him, kept her away for another day. It helped make sure that I wouldn't become the Prophecy One that much sooner.

Instead of answering him, I threw back, "How'd you shatter the chains? In the diner—when they trapped you—you should have been screaming in pain. But you weren't, and then the chains shattered like glass. What'd you do?"

He shook his head, not wanting to tell me. His eyes narrowed to slits as we stared at each other, both wanting information, but neither of us wanting to give it. Finally, he suggested, "A secret for a secret? You tell me and I'll tell you."

"You go first," I replied. I expected to give him what he wanted and get nothing in return. Neither of us trusted the other. And why would we? Eric was terrifying, but I finally had a glimpse of the new Eric, and he was equally afraid of me. I could see it in his eyes, and in the way that he carried himself.

We stared at each other, neither of us making any motion to move. Neither of us had any intention of telling our secrets, but Eric surprised me when his lips parted and he spoke first. "It has something to do with how I was made." His jaw clenched shut, and every muscle in his body flexed. He was enraged that I'd made him what he was. He swallowed hard, and continued, "I'm not a normal Valefar. Celestial silver doesn't affect me the way it does other Valefar. It hurts like hell, but it can't kill me. That's why I wanted you.

That's why I brought you here. I need to know what happened to me in the Lorren."

I hesitated, not wanting to tell him anything, but part of me wanted to come clean. I promised myself that if I had the chance, I would confess what happened in the Lorren. And he answered my question. He shattered the chains because it was something I could do. Without knowing it, I'd made him into a different kind of Valefar—one that was more powerful. Eric watched me as time passed, and all I could do was stare at him willing myself to speak, but not finding the words.

Finally, I broke his gaze, knowing what I would say. I pulled my knees tightly to my chest, and said, "I never intended to kill you. I found you lying on the ground, writhing in pain. Your body was dusted from head to toe with brimstone dust. I knew what it was, because you'd told me about it. That was the first time I'd ever seen it used on someone." I swallowed hard. "I didn't see who did it to you. Since I knew it couldn't hurt me, I tried to comfort you. I was just going to stay with you until you died, but I thought," I opened my mouth, willing the words to come out, but they were stuck in my throat. Eric was hanging on my words, waiting for me to finish. "I thought I could save you. So I gave you a demon kiss. I thought that I could fix you. I thought…" but words wouldn't form.

"You thought that you'd be immune to the allure of the demon kiss, but you weren't—were you?" Eric's words stung. That was the part that haunted me. I could still taste his soul sliding down my throat, and I craved him even more.

"No," I breathed. "I wasn't immune. I'd thought that I'd save you the way I saved…someone else. But, he wasn't hurt the way you were. To make the pain stop, I had to kiss you. I had to take your soul away so you weren't a Martis anymore. I thought if I turned you Valefar, that I could help you. But, I couldn't…" my voice dropped so low I wasn't sure he could hear me. My mouth hung open, as he finished my thought.

"You couldn't stop." Eric's eyes were wide as he watched me. I nodded, unable to speak.

I felt completely naked at that moment, vulnerable, and exposed. That was the worst mistake that I'd ever made, and I was telling Eric. He didn't force me to say it. He didn't put the thoughts in my head. They were always there, swimming at the back of mind, trying to come forward—but I wouldn't let them. I couldn't accept that I'd stolen his soul and enjoyed every second of it.

CHAPTER TWENTY-NINE

The rest of that night was weird. Eric moved around me like a spooked cat. Before then, it was clear that he had control over me, but now he knew that was a façade. I could kill him whenever the urge struck me. Tension was building. I didn't want to leave and face Collin. I couldn't tell Al that I got away from Eric because I became the girl everyone said I'd become. The thought made me want to crawl under a rock and die. Eric didn't try to comfort me. I would have punched him if he tried. I wanted to punish him for making me lust after his blood. Whenever he got too close to me, I'd lose my thoughts and want nothing but for him to give me a taste—a tiny drop of his blood. I fought the longings, but it was impossible to deny. If Eric wanted to give me more of his blood, he could—and I'd eagerly accept.

Finally, Eric broke the silence. "I need to know," he demanded. "You have to tell me what happened in the Lorren."

I looked up at him, "What do you mean; you're not the same as other Valefar?" He'd said it before, but being more powerful and smarter, well, Eric was powerful and smart before. What's the difference?

"I shattered the celestial silver chains. They splintered like cheap glass." He touched his arms, where he still had welt marks from the chains. "The silver can still kill me, it still hurt, but I was able to shatter it. I'm stronger, faster, and you already know I have proficiency with blood."

"So," I asked. "You said all Valefar do." I didn't like him mentioning blood. It made me long for him again. Damn it! Focus Ivy!

"Yeah, but mine's more powerful. And the cost factor seems to be...unusual," he answered. "I can't tell you more than that, but it's enough that I know something's different. I need you to retell what happened the night I died." Eric rose and gestured for me to come. "We're going to a different room."

I got up and followed him. He walked swiftly down an elaborate hallway lined with framed pieces of art. When I recognized that a few of the oil paintings were real, I stopped and blurted out, "Where the hell are we? Did you break into some rich guy's house?"

Eric kept walking, and looked annoyed that I stopped. "Keep moving. And no. He gave it to me. And he's still here." He winked at me over his shoulder, and my stomach turned to ice.

"Where? Eric!" I ran up behind him, and he flinched turning toward me.

He slammed his body into mine and pinned me to the wall. I tried to push him away, thinking he was playing, but he breathed, "Nothing's changed, Taylor. It takes you time to flame out into the psycho chick. Seconds that I could use to kill you." My heart raced as he stared at me with wild eyes. I could feel his heart beating rapidly as he crushed me to the wall. "I know you're still here because you're afraid to tell them what you are. Fine by me, but never think you're safe around me. I intend to make the person who did this to me pay for it tenfold. Even if it turns out to be you..." With that, he pushed off me and continued walking down the hall.

My eyes narrowed to slits as I followed him. What was I doing? Eric was crazy and totally unpredictable. Collin told me as much. And I knew it watching him, but there was something inside of me that couldn't leave. Not yet. I hadn't come to terms with what I'd done. And if I left, I'd have to tell Collin that I turned Eric into a Valefar. And I couldn't bear it. The look on his face would be crushing. No, I had to stay here longer.

The interior of the house was dark. Eric and I slid through the hallways with ease. It seemed like no one else was in the entire house. And it was huge. The enormous windows that would have lit the corridor from the sides and above where obscured by large velvet draperies that stretched to impossible heights. The paintings along the walls kept coming, showcasing a fine art collection that rivaled some museums. The size of the house and the riches within made me think we were in the Hamptons. I didn't bother to ask Eric, because it didn't matter. I could get home by effonating and Collin could heal me. A pang of longing washed over me. I wanted to tell him everything, but I was afraid he wouldn't understand. Or worse.

Eric swung opened a door and stopped, indicating that I should pass him and enter the room. It made me uneasy when I passed him. He glared down at me with an intensity that was difficult to endure. His amber eyes burned into me, and his jaw locked while I passed. The scent of his blood subtly slowed my movements as I passed him. Without thinking my tongue licked my upper lip as I passed him, causing a slight smile to spread across his face.

I looked up at him, realizing what I'd done, and muttered, "You suck."

He smiled back, "Yeah, but I also saved you from yourself." He let the door close and walked across the dark room to a high wing backed chair that was facing away from us. I froze when I realized someone was sitting in it. An old man looked up at me from behind round glasses. His pale skin and slumped form made me think he'd been sitting like this for some time.

"Eric?" I questioned, but he waved a hand at me to shut up. Eyes wide, I watched him cross the room to a small closet. There was a black padlock on the outside of the door. He inserted a key and twisted. The brimstone lock opened in his hands. As he undid the lock from the latch, and I realized that someone powerful was locked in that tiny room. My heart sank into my feet. What if it was Collin? Or Al? And I'd been sitting down the hall with him for hours. Repulsion at my stupidity shot through me. Eric was a Valefar and acted like it. I had to stop thinking he was something else. He completely screwed me. My thoughts shifted back to the closet as he finished unlocking it.

The tall slender white door opened with ease. I expected someone to come charging out, but Eric reached down, and took a tiny hand in his and pulled the person out of the shadows. The tiny hand was attached to a slender arm, on the petite frame of a girl, with silky cinnamon colored hair. My fists balled in fury as I ran to rip her eyes out of her head, and shove her ass through the black mirror permanently.

"You!" she screamed, recognizing me. Shannon turned to fight, instantly contorting her face with rage. "What'd you do to him? You already did enough!" We fought like high school girls, not like warriors. I was so mad at her for turning on me. My fingers wrapped into her long silky hair and I pulled hard, thrusting her head into the beautifully plastered walls. The owner watched the outburst and ensuing chaos placidly, saying nothing. The vacant expression in his eyes was notable, but I didn't realize what it meant yet. At the same moment that Shannon landed her cat claws on my face and started to rip my skin open with her nails, the aroma hit me.

Breathing hard, I stopped and turned instantly. Shannon's movement echoed my own. Heart racing, I stood in front of Eric, wanting what he had. On each forefinger there was one drop of bright red blood. He held it in front of each of us, and used it to slowly lure us away from each other and toward him. My mind was screaming, telling me to leave, to run away, to do anything but follow that beautiful drop of blood on Eric's beautiful fingers. Burning intensity shot through me with longing I've never known. When he stopped moving, I finally looked up at him.

Eric's eyes were wide as he gazed at me. In that second, I wasn't afraid of him. There was something less feral about him, less angry, and more like the old Eric. I forgot about the blood, and stood transfixed until he asked me to sit. I complied without thought, willing to do anything Eric asked of me.

His voice was smooth and sweet, "I have a drop for each of you. All you have to do to get it is answer my questions." He turned to Shannon and my heart fell. I wanted him to talk to me. I wanted his eyes on me, his perfect face turned toward me. But, I heard him ask her, "Were you there with us in the Lorren?" She had a goofy expression on her face and nodded. Eric turned, asking me the same question.

"Yes," I answered eagerly.

I felt so strange. I didn't like Shannon, but I could no longer remember why. The hatred that seared through my veins moments ago was gone. My fixation shifted between Eric's golden eyes and the dark red drop of blood sitting on top of his index finger as he held it up careful not to spill it. I decided that if the drop rolled off his finger, I'd have to get it before it hit the floor. My eyes widened at the thought. I shook my head. It felt like I was encased in a cloud and everything was surreal. Eric moved closer to me, breathing in my ear causing me to shudder. I forgot what I was thinking.

His voice was patient. Apparently he was repeating himself, "Did you throw Brimstone dust on me?" I looked into his golden eyes and shook my head slowly, "No. No, I found you covered in Brimstone. I didn't realize what it was at first. You were in so much pain…" my voice trailed off.

Eric nodded and asked Shannon the same question. She moved slowly, like I did, with wide green eyes eager to please him. "No," she said, "I saw Ivy do it, and leave. When she came back, she kissed you. I couldn't help because I couldn't touch you…but I wanted to. I wanted to help you."

Eric was quiet for a moment, and stared at me. "Did you see the Lorren? Did it hurt you?"

I smiled softly as my head swam. "Lorren is beautiful. He healed me, he didn't hurt me Eric. Why would he do that?"

Eric arched an eyebrow at me, not understanding me. He tried again, "Ivy," he waved the drop of blood under my eyes. I sucked in with delight wanting to taste it and feel it slide against my tongue. "I need to know if the Lorren—the golden maze—made it look like a person appeared when we were separated. Did you see someone who wasn't supposed to be in the maze?"

I laughed, "You're so silly! Of course I did. Collin was there, and then later Lorren was there." I tried to place my hand on Eric's forearm, but he pulled away. Disappointment was clearly visible in my frown.

Shannon's wide green eyes stared at me confused. She asked me, "Why do I know you?" Eric distracted her by waving his finger before her again. She was fighting through the mental haze Eric had cast over us. Maybe it was his blood, maybe it was more than that. Either way I felt giddy and wanted to suck his finger. The thought shocked me and I giggled.

Eric turned to me, "Ivy, did you kill me?"

Surprised he'd ask me, I nodded, "Yes. I gave you a demon kiss. I drank your soul to try to save you." I paused, looking up at him, frowning, trying to remember. "It didn't work. You died anyway."

Eric asked us both a few more questions. Shannon said she saw me kill Eric. She said she tried to avenge his death, but that I overpowered her and sent her through a mirror. He arched an eyebrow at her as she looked up at him adoringly.

"She liked you," I blurted out. "She said I stole you from her. But you were stuck on…" I searched for her name. I could feel it on the tip of my tongue, "Lydia." Eric's amber eyes were wide. "You still loved Lydia. I only reminded you of her. You didn't love me, like Shannon thought."

Eric's voice was odd. I could hear it even through the haze. "Kiss me Ivy. Remember what I told you about Lydia when you do." Ecstatic, I moved to comply. Eric held his hands out to the side, careful not to drop the blood. I was remembering Eric telling me about Lydia and how he tried to save her and failed, and I brushed my lips against his. He shuddered at the touch, and I pulled away. My smile faded when I realized that he wasn't pleased with me. The expression on his face was displeased. He blinked at me, and shook off the expression. Shannon was sitting on the edge of her chair ready to fly out of it if I upset him. Eric held his fingers upright and the blood began to trail down his finger. He said we did well, and offered us each the thing we desired most. Shannon latching onto him until the blood was gone. He asked her to go sit in the closet and she left.

I stared at Eric, watching the drop of blood as it slid down his finger and onto his palm. I wanted it so badly, but I couldn't act. I couldn't do the thing I pictured in my mind…I couldn't slide my tongue over his palm and take what he was offering.

Eric's voice was deep, and commanding, "Take it, Ivy. Do it."

He watched me fight, trying to resist the need that he made me have. Looking up into his eyes, I took a deep breath, and turned away. It felt like someone ripped my arms off. I wanted the drop of blood. I wanted it so badly, but my mind kept telling me not to take it—run. When I felt him press himself to my back, I sucked in a shocked gasp. I was so close to giving in. His left hand slid around my waist and under the hem of my shirt. His warm hand pressed into my skin, pulling me closer to him.

Trembling started to make it impossible to hold body still, and when he spoke softly in my right ear it sent a shiver down my spine. "Drink it," he purred. "You know you want it, Ivy. Drink it, and be in bliss… I'll give you anything you want. Anything…"

His lips pressed against my neck and an explosion of butterflies erupted in my stomach. A moan escaped me as his fingers lifted and touched the tiny drop of blood to my lips. I closed my eyes, fighting it. The blood was right there. It was all I wanted. That tiny drop contained instant bliss. All I had to do was open my mouth and taste it.

Heart racing wildly, part of me wanted me to break free of his hold and run. That part recognized how dangerous Eric was. In in the back of my mind, I was screaming, terrified. But somewhere else, I realized what had drawn me to Eric; why I stayed when I could have left, why I was thrilled when he touched me, and why I was having so much trouble fighting him off—I liked him. On some level, I always have. And now, he was impossible to resist with his hands stretched across on my stomach, his lips pressed to my neck, and his blood so close to my mouth.

Turning slowly in his arms, I looked up at him. My lips parted as I whispered, "No."

CHAPTER THIRTY

I expect him to scream, but he just smiled at me. His fingers slid off my waist and he wiped his hand off on his dark jeans, before walking over to Shannon's closet to lock her back inside. My heart was racing as he walked away. Staring at his back, I wondered what was wrong with me. Did I really like him? How could that happen? I loved Collin. Convinced that it must be something that Eric was doing to me, I didn't worry about it too much. For some reason, Eric didn't force me to take his blood.

Before we left the room, he gave the old man food and put a drop of his blood on the man's cup. He picked up the glass and obediently licked it clean. I cringed inside. Watching someone else take what I wanted was unnerving. I looked over at Eric. "What are you doing with them? Are they part of your collection or something? I thought you were going to kill Shannon," I asked. "Why did you lock her up?" I wrapped my arms around my middle to ward off the cold.

Eric's gaze cut back to me unconcerned, "They wronged me. This is their punishment."

I swallowed hard, knowing I'd been lumped in with them. "When you left me in Hell, you said you were going to kill whoever did this to you. Why are they still alive?"

Eric rounded on me outside the door. "You'd be dead now if I did what I'd originally planned." He turned away from me, "Besides," he smiled over his shoulder, "there's more than one way to destroy a person."

My throat constricted as I watched the evil smile fade off his face. I decided it was time to leave; time for me to leave and face whatever was coming next. Losing Al and Collin's trust wasn't something I wanted, but I thought I had to tell them. No matter what I felt about Eric, aligning myself with him would be insane. He was collecting people and feeding them blood. Shannon was happily living in a closet. I wondered who else he had trapped in this big old house. No, it was time to go, but I had to find out what I'd originally wanted to know.

I followed him back to the white room, where he closed the door behind me. His voice was strange, "I didn't think you could resist me." I turned to him and shrugged, not wanting to discuss it. I remembered how eager I was to please him when he had a drop of blood on his finger. It shamed me, and I felt my face grow hot thinking about how I was all too delighted to kiss him when he asked. Thinking back, that part seemed weird. I looked over at him wondering why he did that. He only asked me to kiss him. And that had nothing to do with the Lorren. My brows knitted together as I thought about it. "What's that look on your face," Eric asked.

I turned and looked up at him, asking, "Why'd you ask me to kiss you?" I asked it without feeling—the same way you'd ask for someone to save you a table or grab your mail.

Eric arched a brow and moved closer to me. He liked trying to use his body to intimidate me. He didn't realize that I thought he looked nice and really didn't mind. "What's it matter?"

I shrugged, "Just thought it didn't line up with the rest of your questions. And I would have told you that stuff anyway. There wasn't any need to do whatever you did."

Eric smiled crookedly, "You would have? Just as quickly and without question?" He laughed and turned away, "I don't think so."

Defiance rose up inside of me. If he acted normal—like Eric—I would have answered his questions. I grabbed his arm and turned him back toward me. We stood nose to nose. "Try me." It wasn't a choice.

"Kiss me, Taylor," his lips turned up at the corners as his eyes bore into mine. "Kiss me like you need me. Like you want me. Open your lips for me, and think of me—think of the Eric you knew before I died." His arms were folded across his chest. He leaned down while talking to me, so that all my senses were going nuts. Normally, I would have never done it... but this time I did.

Without a second's hesitation, I reached out and took his face between my palms and pulled him to me. I swept my tongue over his lips once, and when they parted I kissed him deeply, knowing that he could take my soul any time he damn well pleased. Maybe it was insanity; maybe I had more issues than I thought. Either way, it was reckless. Collin and I never said anything about cheating, but he'd be pissed if he knew I willingly kissed Eric. I pushed back the thoughts as I focused on the thing Eric requested.

Little things shot into my mind, along with the big things—the fights, the tears I shed when I thought he killed Apryl, how I didn't really blame him for her death even though that wasn't what I told him. I thought about who he was and how I didn't mind his hands on my body, or his lips on mine. Breathless, I pulled away from him determined to get the information I needed.

He licked his lips, and gasped, "Thank you."

I nodded, not knowing what he was thanking me for. Jumping straight to my question, I asked, "How much of your old life do you remember, Eric?" He winced and turned from me, but I grabbed his arm and wouldn't let him walk away. "I just did what you wanted, no questions asked. You need to return the favor."

He smirked, "Fine," he folded his arms looking down at me. "What do you want?"

Hope swelled in my chest. I reached into my pocket and unfolded a page. I had copied it from the book when no one was paying attention. Al and Collin thought it was a bad idea to take the book with me, so I didn't. I only took one page and didn't tell them about it. I pressed the page into his hands.

"Read it to me."

Puzzled, he looked down at the crinkled paper, and smoothed it out. Walking over to a desk, he put it down and ran his finger over it. After a minute, he shook his head. "I don't know. It's coded or something." He crumpled it and threw it back to me.

"No! You have to read it!" I yelled, smoothing the paper again and thrusting it at him. He wouldn't take it back and just turned to look at me. There was no bond with Eric, nothing to tap into to see what he was feeling, but something had changed in the past few hours. He didn't go back to being the evil monster again. He stayed trapped somewhere in the middle. "I know you read it." I saw the flick of his eyes once he identified the pattern. I didn't think he wouldn't tell me... Especially if it didn't matter.

"Maybe I did," he said, shirking off the paper. "So what? You don't need what's on there. Go suck your boyfriend's soul out and get your life back."

What did he just say? Shock washed over me as my heart pounded in my chest. He knew what we were trying to do? He knew everything. But how? I stared at him in disbelief with my mouth hanging open. And, he could read that page, too. Too stunned to speak, I watched as Eric sat down in the chair and kicked his boots up onto the desk. He stretched, putting his hands behind his neck. The neck I almost severed...

Completely, frustrated, I made a face. "If you can read it, why won't you tell me? I need to know what it says."

Eric looked at me, his face expressionless. "It doesn't tell you what you want to know. Bring me the rest of the book and I'll find it for you." With that he shot out of the chair and left me alone.

CHAPTER THIRTY-ONE

Effonating sucks. Before I completely lost my mind and willingly elected to stay with Eric, I left. When he wouldn't read the page to me, I left it on his desk and wrote on top of it. The message was stupid, embarrassing really. I scrawled, I still believe in you. As if I had any reason to. Deranged and homicidal weren't two of my favorite characteristics in a friend, but apparently, it was growing easier to overlook terrible shortcomings.

When I appeared back at St. Bart's, several days had passed. I fell on the kitchen floor, screaming, with more skin spliced off my body than last time. Al found me first, with Collin right on her heels. I was quickly doused in the mixture to ease the pain. After the skin regrew, I felt weak, but had enough strength to talk. I told them some things, and intentionally left out other things…like my new Eric addiction.

When I awoke, I realized that strange dreams didn't plague me. Slowly, my eyes opened and I noticed that Collin held me in his arms. He pushed back a stray curl and said, "You seemed restless. I held you for a while, and chased off the dreams that usually plague you." His fingers brushed the hair away from my face as he looked at me. "It's kinda weird to be in bed with a hot girl in a church with a nun who doesn't seem to mind." He smiled at me.

I laughed and sat up, feeling awkward—and guilty for kissing Eric. I don't know if I was truly attracted to Eric, or if was because of his blood. Looking at Collin, I felt sad.

He lounged on his side, on my bed, and looked up at me. A black tee shirt clung to his chest, revealing perfectly sculpted arms. Dark hair fell into his eyes as he leaned toward me, asking softly, "What happened?"

I told him most of the story, leaving some things out. Collin hated Eric when he was a Martis, but now that he was a Valefar, his dislike turned to seething hatred. As I was talking about Eric, the bond was in turmoil. Collin was trying to hide his feelings, but the more I spoke about Eric, the worse it got. I left out the kisses, not wanting to cause him anymore pain. But I wondered if that counted as cheating on him. I was afraid that if I had to ask that question, then it was.

"So, he read the page?" Collin asked, shocked. "How? How did he remember it?"

I shrugged, "I don't know. But he won't tell me what it says without the rest of the book."

"Of course not," Collin mumbled. "No doubt he's going to steal the book and go after Satan's Stone himself."

I straightened, "I don't think so. It's hard to get a read on Eric, but he seemed like he couldn't be bothered with this stuff. It sounded more like a favor, for me." I looked up at Collin and realized that was the worst thing I could have said.

He asked me, "Did he do anything to you? You may not have noticed before, but that guy has always wanted you."

I smiled, not believing Eric wanted me at all before, and took his hands between mine. "I'm fine. He didn't hurt me. But I need this. Please, Collin? Please let me bring him the rest of the book. We can copy the pages so we have them too—in case he does something stupid." I looked up into his eyes, pleading with him.

He looked away from me. "Whenever Eric is around, bad things happen to you. I don't want you involved this time. Let me or Al do it, all right?" I agreed. It was the best I could get. I just hoped Eric would behave and do what he said he would do.

CHAPTER THIRTY-TWO

Al took the large leather book to the center of the clearing at the old park. Trees surrounded the wide field, jutting up jagged, leafless branches into the night sky. Eric didn't choose this place, we did. It made us think that things would at least partly go in our favor, but everything fell apart that night. Thinking about it makes me shiver. It was so obvious, but I never saw it coming.

Al held the book between her ancient hands waiting to see the boy she raised as her own—the boy she'd kill without an instant of hesitation if she had to. I wasn't a Martis and I was glad I wasn't. I didn't understand them at all. Everyone made me think the next time I saw Shannon that she would best me if I gave her the chance, but she was a mindless blood junkie living in Eric's closet, waiting for her next fix. It angered me that Eric tried to do the same thing to me, but he wasn't able to. That was the only reason I got away from him. But the words he said when he shattered the silver chains and stole me from the diner echoed in my mind, *She's mine.* He could have said a million different things, but that was what he chose to say. On some level now, I knew that I would always be his. I'd crave him and long for him in ways that made me feel torn inside. I pushed the thought away, too upset to deal with it right then.

I looked over at Collin. We were waiting for Al, under the trees about not too far away. We were close enough to see, but we wouldn't be able to hear her. I sat on top of a worn out wood picnic table with Collin sitting opposite me on top of another table. A question I forgot to ask crossed my mind. Now wasn't really the right time to ask, but we were alone, and I didn't want Al to hear. I watched the old woman, standing defiantly in the field. Waiting.

I asked softly, "Why didn't you tell me about the blood?" Collin glanced up, startled by my question. His leather jacket was hanging open, and he shoved his hands into the pockets. "Why didn't you tell me that Valefar blood had an addicting quality? That Eric would be able to mesmerize me like that? I don't see why you hid that from me…"

Collin stared at me as I asked, and shook his head. "Ivy, we can't talk about this now. We need to watch Al in case she needs us. I don't like you being here at all." Collin kept looking around; acting like something was going to happen.

Irritation shot through me. He was hiding something from me, and I wished he weren't. I glanced back up at Collin, not wanting to drop it. "He trapped me so easily because you didn't tell me something…something that you already knew."

Collin's blue eyes were stormy. He leaned forward on his elbows, hands clasped together. "You didn't need to know that. The odds of him doing that to you with his blood were miniscule. You didn't tell me that before. I didn't realize he'd done it to you before." He was angry.

I slid off the picnic table and walked over to him. Moonlight shone through the branches forming jagged patterns on the ground. "Why are we hiding things from each other? Just tell me, Collin." I placed my hands over his. "You knew, didn't you? You knew that Valefar blood can do that? He has Shannon locked in a closet, begging for more. It gave him control over me that I didn't think he had."

Collin jumped up, pushing me away. "It's never that severe. Valefar blood should have never trapped you. It just makes you crave it, and want more—more of the person who gave it. It makes you lust after it when it's gone. It does that to pure Martis. You aren't a pure Martis. Its effect on you should be miniscule." He shook his head, folding his arms close to his chest as he looked down at me. "Eric's stronger than I thought. He's stronger than any of us thought." He glanced back at Al sharply, and then at me. He was shaking his head, "This is a bad idea, Ivy. This is a trap. It has to be. He doesn't want the book. He's coming after you."

Exasperated, I sighed and shook my head. "He had me Collin. He could have made me stay, but he didn't. I didn't escape… He let me leave." The expression on Collin's face changed from fear to shock. His wide eyes were impossibly blue as he reached for me, wrapping his fingers around my wrist.

He said, "We need to leave. Now!" Panic spilled across Collin's face as his gaze cut between Al and me, looking for Eric.

But I jerked away from him. "No. Tell me first. Tell me now! Why didn't you say anything to me about his blood?" I stared up into Collin's eyes. His mouth hung open, like he wanted to tell me but no words would come out.

The voice came from behind a tree standing right in front of us. "I know why." Eric moved from the shadows and came into the little clearing filled with tables. "Want me to tell her?"

Collin moved in front of me quickly, as if he thought Eric might hurt me. But Eric laughed. "Ivy can choose whoever she wants. Some days she wants you. Some days she wants me..." Eric said, talking calmly, while he walked in circles us.

My heart was caught in my throat. I watched as he paced around us, unsure of what he was doing. Collin turned his body, pushing me behind him as Eric circled us. He was trying to keep him away from me.

"This isn't your place," Collin growled through his teeth. "Leave before I make you." Every muscle in Collin's body was tense, and ready to fight.

Eric stopped pacing and his golden eyes lingered on me as Collin stood in front of me. His voice was seductive, "Ask your question, Ivy. I have the answers. I'm not trying to be something I'm not. I don't pretend with you, and you know it. There's a simple reason why he didn't tell you about the blood... there's a simple reason why you're so enamored with him..." Eric's eyes gleamed.

I looked up at Collin, not following what Eric was saying, "What's he talking about?" I laughed as if what Eric was saying couldn't possibly be true. "He didn't feed me his blood. That isn't why I love him." Those sentences began as statements. I was telling Eric that he was wrong, but as I finished speaking I could barely breathe.

Watching the expression in Collin's eyes—I saw something that made me question him. "Collin?" I looked up at him. His jaw was tense, as he gazed over my head at Eric with hatred. When he looked back down at me, my stomach twisted as all the air was crushed from my lungs. "You didn't?" My voice trembled as I asked him, but I already knew the answer. Disbelief engulfed me. It couldn't be true. It couldn't be! I used the bond, expecting it to tell me that Collin loved me and would never do something like feed me demon blood. I pushed into him with my mind and was overwhelmed with feelings of regret. Wide-eyed, he stood in front of me unable to hide it any longer.

My heart sank as I felt my eyes sting, "When?" I breathed and slapped my hand against his chest. But Collin stood there, saying nothing, neither confirming nor denying my questions. He didn't have to. The bond filled with remorse so deep that I nearly doubled over in pain.

Horror filled me, as looked up into Collin's face. My fists beat against his chest as tears streaked my face, "When? When did you do this to me? And why didn't you tell me that what I felt for you was from your blood! Why didn't you tell me you made me addicted to you! All this time, I thought you loved me. I thought I loved you! How could you?" I shrieked as Collin failed to answer me. His lips pressed tightly together, as he struggled to speak, and more silence lingered between us. I smashed my fists into his chest harder this time, wanting to hurt him.

He grabbed my wrists gently finally, saying, "Ivy, it wasn't like that. The blood does have that effect—it can make you enamored with me—but you liked me before all that happened. It wasn't like that. It wasn't. Please believe me…" He dropped my hands, and held my face to make me look up at him. His bright blue eyes were terrified. The bond was overwhelming me with fear…he was afraid he'd lose me.

I pushed him away, feeling like his words tore a hole in my stomach. Unable to accept what he did, I asked, "When? Why don't I remember it?" Collin stepped toward me, reaching for me, but I stepped away. I wouldn't let him come any closer. His touch, his voice, his scent—they could all be used to manipulate me.

Eric moved towards us, shoving his hands in his pockets. I'd forgotten he was there. When he spoke up, he surprised us both, saying, "It was the night you almost died, Ivy. When I found you in the woods, I could smell it. His blood was on your lips. It wasn't Jake's." Shock silenced Collin and I. Eric wasn't supposed to remember his previous life, but he remembered that. He remembered all of it. Before I could ask anything else, he kept going, moving closer and closer to me. "He gave you a little blood that night, to save you of course." Eric looked at Collin, with a lazy smile on his face, "And maybe you gave her a little later, when she didn't recover from a vision the way you wanted. You told her that you threw water on her, but water didn't affect her—but blood would. Anything like that happen, Ivy?"

My stomach was sinking as it twisted tighter and tighter. My heart was racing, hammering inside my head. The more Eric said, the larger the crushing fear that Collin was using me this entire time grew. I looked at Collin wondering if I knew him at all. He had doused me with water one night when I had a vision. I was soaking wet when I came to. He said he had to pull me out of a vision, and that he was worried something had happened to me. It was possible that he fed me more blood that night. I was unconscious and didn't actually see what he did. Did he? Did he feed me his blood to pull me out of the vision like that? Remembering back, Collin looked terrified. Was it possible that he did it? Looking into his face, I wanted him to deny it. I wanted him to say it never happened, but he didn't.

The bond swirled memories at me, memories laced with regret. Some of the thoughts were mine and some were his. I pushed through the haze trying to latch onto what I knew from the night Jake attacked me. I died. I felt my soul trying to leave my body. Most of it was devoured, but I suddenly wondered why Jake stopped. The memories from that night were so cloudy. Was it possible that Collin had demon kissed me, too? Repulsion and shock made my mouth fall open as fear ripped through my body.

"Ivy," Collin pleaded, "don't listen to him. He's lying. That's not what happened. I would never..." he reached for me, but I backed away from him. My mouth was hanging open and no matter what I did, I couldn't push past the shock. Why would he do this to me? Why would Collin use demon blood like this on me? If his words were true, if we liked each other before, why did he do it?

Eric strode between us and cut him off, "You'd never... what? Never want her to know the truth? Never want her to know how much you wanted her, when she didn't want you. Blood kinda changes that, doesn't it? Now she can't stop thinking about you. Now she wants you even if she doesn't know why." Eric looked back at me. I couldn't speak. Every inch of my body felt like it was going to rip apart. When Eric smiled at me, I knew it was going to get worse. He turned back to Collin, asking, "But what about you? You'd never want to know what secrets she's been hiding from you?"

Turning sharply toward Eric, my stomach went cold. "Eric, don't!" But it was too late. Nothing I said or did could have stopped what happened next. I watched in horror as the last bits of my world were torn apart.

"Ask her how many times she kissed me," Eric said. He walked next to me, but I couldn't look at him. I couldn't make him stop. I wanted to flee, but he grabbed my arm and spoke calmly to Collin like this conversation didn't bother him in the least.

Collin's gaze shifted between us, suddenly thinking we'd been more than friends. Tears were streaming down my face as I said, "Collin, no! Don't listen to him!"

Collin's voice was faint, "Is he lying? You kissed him? More than once?" Collin shook his head. His eyes were wide, and tore into me in a way only Collin could do.

I opened my mouth to answer—to tell him that it wasn't like that. That I'd never hurt him, but Eric cut me off. I gazed at Eric, willing him to stop, but he didn't. It felt like every stitch that held me together was unraveling, and all I could manage was to stand there and watch. Power is useless unless you use it, and at that moment I was utterly powerless.

Eric nodded, "Several times, actually. And in the Lorren, did you tell him about that, Ivy? Did you tell him that you gave me a special kiss—a demon kiss. Did you tell him that you made me what I am? Does he know that you were the one who stole my soul?"

The bond erupted. Anger poured through it in uncontrollable waves. Collin rounded on me, but Eric stood between us. He wouldn't let Collin get closer.

Collin screamed, "You turned him Valefar! You gave him a demon kiss? How could you? How could you do something so evil after I've told you everything?" He reached for me again. I couldn't fight back. I didn't try to defend myself. As far as I was concerned, he was right. Tears streaked my face. This couldn't be happening. I cowered behind Eric unable to speak. "Ivy, answer me!" Collin roared.

But I had no answers. I couldn't tell Collin what I'd done to Eric. I couldn't admit the fascination I'd had as I drank Eric's soul. I couldn't do it.

Eric stood next to me and assured him calmly, "It wasn't the way you think. I only told you because you two have been lying to each other. Come clean and pick up the pieces." His words were lies. I could hear it in his voice. He meant for this to happen. He took everything he knew and used it against me.

I looked up at Eric with a tearstained face. The winter wind bit at my cheeks, but I didn't care. "I trusted you. You were supposed to read the book and go."

Collin was still fuming, but when Eric grabbed for me, he stepped between us. Collin shoved me back and I was out of Eric's reach. Eric leaned toward me, narrowly evading Collin's fist, and said sternly, "I told you—never trust a Valefar."

I pushed past Collin, walking up to Eric and screaming in his face, "How could you possibly remember that? What did you do?" He told me that months ago, when he was a Martis.

Eric only smiled at me, saying, "It wasn't me, Ivy. It was you." His body turned to mist and disappeared. I looked up at Collin, shocked for a moment, without realizing what was about to happen. Across the field there was a surge of pure blue light as Al held the book in one arm and threw a blast of light at her former student. Eric danced around her with ease, snapping brimstone chains on a short black stick at her hands. He was trying to get the book.

Collin and I stared at each other. Without another word, I took off as fast my feet could go. Efanonting would peel my skin off and weaken me. It wasn't an option. But, I had to get there now. Collin's figure disappeared from my side, and reappeared behind Eric. Collin didn't have celestial silver with him to kill Eric. And I was the only one who knew it wouldn't work. Al didn't know. I never had the chance to tell her. Eric was immune to for some reason, and the reason had to do with me. It didn't matter what they did to him—Eric would win. My heart was about to tear my chest in two as I ran at them, so close but still too far away to stop them.

There was a matter of seconds before Eric took the book from Al. The old woman never faltered once in her life. She instantly melded balls of light and sent them crashing into Eric. Eric staggered, but he resumed his attack every single time. Collin and Al closed in on him, thinking they had him. But they didn't know.

My feet pounded towards them as I screamed, "No!" But it was too late.

When the nun pulled out her silver weapon, it took the shape of a cutlass with a single shining blade made for decapitation. She swung it at Eric, and hit her mark, but as the blade came into contact with Eric's neck it shattered. A million pieces of celestial silver fragments glittered in the air as they exploded from Al's weapon. Collin backed away as the lethal substance flew in every direction.

Momentarily stunned, Al's mouth dropped open as her blade disintegrated in her hand. She paused as the weapon turned to dust. Eyes wide, she looked up at Eric with terror in her eyes. Eric jumped behind the old woman and with a flick of his wrist, caught the brimstone chains in his other hand, slid it under her throat—and pulled. The book fell to the ground as the brimstone blackened chains sliced through her neck. Al's body crumpled and fell to the ground.

Screaming rang in my ears as I watched what happened, unable to help. My heart lurched in my chest when I saw Al's body fall. Every muscle in my body screamed to go faster and stop him before he escaped. Collin paused for only half a second after the shards landed, but it was too long. He dove at Eric. Eric had already snatched the book from the dust. While he did so, Eric held his golden gaze locked on mine with a smirk on his face.

During those seconds, it felt like time stopped. I couldn't run fast enough. It didn't matter that my hair had turned to violet flames, and my power crackled around me. It didn't matter that I never slowed. It didn't matter that my power came when I needed it, because it was already too late. Violet flames crackled from my fingertips as I reached for Eric's neck. He would never walk away from me ever again. The violet flames licked his skin, but Eric effonated, and his body dissolved before I could rip him to pieces. I fell to the ground, next to the place where Al lay motionless. Screams of rage ravaged my throat as I beat the dirt with my hands next to her.

When I looked up, Collin stood next to me. His face was dirty, and bleeding. He looked at me with my flaming hair whipping around me face. There was a moment when I saw him and he saw me. He knew who I was. He knew the power I had—the power that I had that I was afraid to use. In that moment, my world shattered. Nothing would ever be the same again. Breathing heavily, I looked down at Al. My throat tightened, and I doubled over and buried my face in the dirt, screaming.

Collin tried to pull me up, telling me to leave her there, but I wouldn't let him.

Collin was a traitor. He betrayed me when he fed me his blood. I could never trust him again. But I would lust after him forever because of what he did. All this time, I thought he offered me love, but that wasn't what it was at all. He was no better than Eric.

Eyes wide with rage, I looked up at him. My hostile thoughts pushed into his mind, *The bond's a bitch when the person on the other end hates you, huh?*

Collin's brow pinched tightly with his blue eyes blazing. He went to say something, but snapped his mouth shut. The muscle in his jaw was flexed, as he bit back whatever he was going to say.

I bit off the words, practically spitting in his face, "I never want to see you again." Collin stared at me stonily and didn't reply. He pressed his lips together, as his fingers balled into fists at his sides. I didn't care if I hurt him at that point. The damage was done and there was no way to fix it. He would always mistrust me, and I couldn't look at him without wondering if my feelings for him were real or induced by his blood. Closing my eyes hard, I tore my gaze away from him. Tears streaked my face in an endless wave. I sat next to Al crying into the dirt, and the next time I looked back— Collin was gone.

CHAPTER THRITY-THREE

I went to Al's church to pack my things. I wouldn't be returning there again. Julia would soon learn of Al's death and send someone to replace her. I stuffed some clothes into my bag, and went to the kitchen to pack some food. The night Al died did something to me. It felt like I was torn in half. I sat there until the dim rays of morning shone through the grey clouds and found out the hard way what happens to an ancient Martis' body when they die. I'd had her hand in mine, and was telling her I didn't know what to do. That still I needed her. She was the only one who hadn't lied to me, and now she was gone. As I was pleading and crying, her body turned to white mist in my hands. I watched the pearly vapors as they wisped away from me and into the sky. That was a few hours ago. I managed to pull myself together long enough to decide what to do next.

I went back to the church to pack my things and grab supplies before the other Martis arrived. After ravaging the cabinets, and filling my bag with food, I headed out into the frosty early morning air. The cold gust blew against my face as white specs of tiny snow fell from the sky.

The last time I had to deal with death, I didn't know what to do. Overwhelming sadness had engulfed me then. I allowed it and mourned Apryl for months, doing nothing to avenge her death. I let misery and grief consume me whole until there was nothing left of the girl I'd been. Well, this time would be different. This time, I saw who killed Al and he wasn't getting away from me. This time I knew exactly how to make myself feel better. This time, when I found Eric, I wouldn't let him escape—I'd kill him.

H.M. WARD

SATAN'S STONE

Book #4 in the Demon Kissed Series

Coming

January 10, 2012

If you love the DEMON KISSED series and can't wait for more, visit with over 40,000 fans on facebook:
Facebook.com/DemonKissed

Or the official website:
DemonKissed.com

OTHER BOOKS BY H.M. WARD

DEMON KISSED

CURSED

SATAN'S STONE

Coming January 2012

Demon Kissed

by H.M. Ward

Markings & Scars

field notes on Valefar and Martis
with illustrations

figure 1

New Martis Mark

a pale blue glittery streak indicates a new
Martis - they are most vulnerable now

figure 2

Mature Martis Mark

a bright blue mark darkens above the right
brow on mature Martis

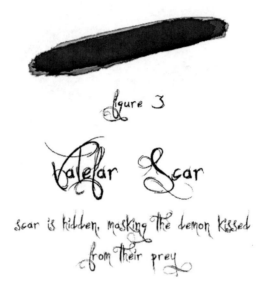

figure 3

Valefar Scar

scar is hidden, masking the demon kissed
from their prey